Mills & Boon Classics

A chance to read and collect some of the best-loved novels from Mills & Boon – the world's largest publisher of romantic fiction.

Every month, four titles by favourite Mills & Boon authors will be re-published in the *Classics* series.

Sara Seale

THE YOUNGEST BRIDESMAID

MILLS & BOON LIMITED
LONDON · TORONTO

This edition 1976

This edition © Sara Seale 1976

ISBN 0 263 72119 1

Made and Printed in Great Britain by
C. Nicholls & Company Ltd
The Philips Park Press, Manchester

CHAPTER ONE

THE wedding dress had been unpacked and hung in splendid isolation in one of the empty guest rooms. The youngest bridesmaid stood gazing with awe at the shimmering folds of velvet, the trimmings of white mink, the rich simplicity of a fairy-tale creation for a winter's bride.

Melissa would look beautiful, she thought, without envy, and her own unexpected part in this modern pageantry once again overwhelmed her with an innocent wonder that she, with her two small feet set so firmly on the ground, should have been thrust haphazardly into a fantasy, for fantasy it was. The Chailey cousins had lived in another world; cards had been sent at Christmas if they remembered, and sometimes she filled in at the last moment for a defaulting guest. She was filling in now for the bridesmaid who had so inconsiderately contracted mumps, and none of it was quite real.

"Lou! Lou!" a voice was calling somewhere in the house.

Voices frequently called, sometimes persuasively, more often impatiently, quite often cross, but this was Cousin Blanche's voice, and not to be ignored, for to her the youngest bridesmaid owed not only her dress and a participation in the most fashionable wedding of the year, but a fortnight's respite from office routine to live under the same roof and make herself generally useful.

"I'm here, Cousin Blanche," she called, and Melissa's mother opened the door with an irritable thrust.

"For heaven's sake, child, why do I have to hunt all over the house for you?" she exclaimed impatiently. "There are a hundred and one jobs you could be doing while we're waiting for the other bridesmaids."

"Are we waiting for them?" Lou asked anxiously, trying

to keep pace with the last few days. The house seemed always to be in the state of waiting for something or someone, fittings, hairdressers, florists, caterers, bridesmaids and, often as not, a truant bride.

"Had you forgotten we've got a rehearsal? Really, Lou, you might pay attention to what you're here for. Why are you mooning up here by yourself?"

"I was admiring the dress. I wanted to see it the moment it was unpacked. It's so beautiful, Cousin Blanche, like a dress made for a fairy-tale princess – but then it's all rather like a fairy tale, isn't it?"

"H'm ... for you, perhaps," Blanche Chailey observed a little dryly, and advanced into the room to examine the dress. Even hanging limply from its padded hanger, its lines had the beauty of expensive simplicity. "Not bad at all, even at the price. I'm glad Melissa was persuaded out of that rather vulgar design she fancied, but Piers, of course, has excellent taste."

"Piers?" Lou looked startled. "But the bridegroom doesn't choose the bridal dress, surely?"

"Why not, since he's paying for it?"

"Oh!"

"Does that rub the bloom off your fairy tale? Piers is a very rich young man and can afford to splash, and you must have gathered by now that we haven't a bean – or did you think all these years that the Chaileys were numbered among the idle rich?"

Lou had. As long as she could remember the Chailey cousins had lived in a separate world, a world Lou's parents had never aspired to. Cousin Blanche, thirty years ago, had been a noted beauty, fêted and spoilt, a legendary rich relation whose path seldom crossed that of her poor relations. In her fifties Blanche still preserved her beauty with every aid that diet and cosmetics could give; her daughter, so very like her, looked in certain lights not a great deal younger.

6

"Well, did you?" Blanche's fine eyes were cynically amused as Lou did not speak.

"Well, yes, I suppose so."

"And now you know better? Oh, my dear child, you needn't imagine I don't know the gossip that's going around. The other bridesmaids talk, don't they? Jealous of Melissa, of course, which is natural – Piers has been the despair of ambitious mamas for years. Did they resurrect ancient history for you, too?"

"How you were once engaged to Piers' father, you mean?"

"And threw him over at the last minute for a rich man old enough to be my father? I did, you know. It was one of life's little ironies that later Piers' father should inherit that vast, very unexpected fortune, and my extremely dull husband should lose his in some City swindle. Sounds like a cheap novelette, doesn't it? The wheel is turning full circle."

"How?"

"Piers is a romantic at heart – so unrewarding these materialistic days. He never quite forgot, you see."

"Forgot?"

"Didn't you know his father was a widower at the time I was engaged to him? Piers, as a small boy, had a thing about me – put me in the place of his own mother, I suppose. I think he has some crazy notion that in marrying Melissa he's putting things right."

"But, Cousin Blanche, that's – that's absolute nonsense!" Lou was so unusually emphatic that her cousin gave her a more attentive glance.

"You think he's in love with my daughter, do you?" she said on a faint note of amusement.

"Of course – besides, I shouldn't think young men make those kinds of gestures."

"Of course! You're very simple, Lou, and rather tediously unworldly."

7

"Very likely," Lou replied with that grave, unexpected air of censure that could sometimes make for discomfort. "I was brought up simply by unworldly parents, but they taught me values, I think, before they died. Does – does that sound – smug, Cousin Blanche?"

"Yes, it does rather," her cousin replied coolly, but she, gave the girl a brief, appraising look. Little Louise Parsons remembered only when she could be useful, had some vague quality that Blanche recognized from her own childhood when life had been more simple and no hint of the human rat-race had clouded her awakening desires. The child, of course, would strike a wrong note in Melissa's retinue of smart young lovelies, but all the same ... all the same, she thought with surprise, she could show them up, too. Lou might have none of the tricks and assurance of Melissa's fashionable friends, but she had something that the others hadn't. What? thought Blanche, frowning, and assessed again the dubious attractions of the young cousin who possessed so few recommendations to present day distinction. Solemn, wide-wake eyes, set far apart in a face too small for them, soft straight brown hair with a fringe, and a long, fragile neck; nothing there to stir the pulses, except, perhaps, her stillness. In an age of restless activity, that stillness could possibly be an asset, Blanche thought uneasily, then wondered at her own disquiet. Why, in the satisfactory culmination of her hopes and schemes, should she be disconcerted by the unspoken censure of an insignificant little kinswoman who had only been roped in from dire necessity?

Lou, uncomfortable under this sudden appraisal, moved away, and her cousin noticed with this unfamiliar, new-found perspicacity the unconscious grace with which the child moved. Louise Parsons worthy of a second glance? Blanche thought impatiently, and spoke with more sharpness than she had intended.

"You must learn to avoid smugness, my dear," she said.

"It doesn't attract sympathy – or the young men."

"No, Cousin Blanche," Lou said with her eyes downcast but Blanche thought she detected a faint gleam through the thick lashes.

"Have you any young men?" she enquired idly, and laughed when the girl did not reply. "Poor Lou – that was an unfair question, I suppose," she said graciously. "You haven't had much chance of meeting eligible admirers, I imagine, but still, you're only nineteen – twenty, is it? You mustn't let Melissa's good fortune sour you."

"Why should it sour me?"

"Well, my dear, let's face it. Piers is rather the Prince Charming of the story books, isn't he? Besides, I think you've lost your heart to him a little, haven't you?"

Lou coloured, deeply and uncharacteristically, and the older woman, who had not intended her remark to be taken in any seriousness, made a small grimace of exasperation.

"My dear child, be your age!" she exclaimed impatiently. "Piers has had more girls in and out of love with him than he can count. You'd only be following the pattern."

The girl's colour faded as quickly as it had come and she replied with a sedate composure that added to her cousin's annoyance:

"Naturally. He's been quite a catch for a good many years, hasn't he? Personally, I find him a little alarming and – and rather too sure of himself."

"Really? But he's scarcely noticed you, has he?"

No, he had scarcely noticed her, and why should he, thought Lou, amongst the other smart and sophisticated bridesmaids who, in their turn, had given her no second thoughts. She spoke only the truth when she declared she found Piers Merrick alarming, and had she not heard his voice before seeing him she might even have disliked him. She had heard him in the hall asking for Melissa, and the unfamiliar voice was warm and somehow tender, and she

9

had caught herself thinking: "That is a voice one could fall in love with."

The voice, she had found on meeting him, was a complete contradiction. His dark face, lined perhaps in an early maturity, was the face of a man who had lived his life and found mostly disillusionment, and his glance when it rested on a woman was at once questing and calculating and soon diverted. He had no real pretensions to good looks but carried a faint air of raffish distinction. She could, Lou had thought, watching and listening in the background, believe there was something of truth in the gossip columns which for so long had bandied his name about, stopping just short of scandal, for the Merrick whims were notorious. His yacht, his racing cars, the island, purchased it was said to satisfy a feudal desire for power, were symbols of a success in which women must have shared from time to time, and Lou experienced a moment's distaste for the willingness of her own sex to accept such carelessly proffered crumbs in order to boast of a temporary conquest. He was spoilt, and indifferent to possible heartaches in others, she had decided with the confidence of youth, then suddenly he had focussed his attention on her and she had the uncomfortable feeling that he knew quite well what she was thinking.

"Our youngest bridesmaid has a disapproving air. Are you finding yourself out of your depth, Cinderella?"

She had felt herself flushing at his tone. Was it so obvious, then, that she was the poor relation, stepping in to fill a tiresome gap, or was he simply taunting her for forming unwarrantable conslusions? But her eyes met his steadily across the room and she sat with her hands still demurely folded in her lap, beating down her embarrassment.

"No," she replied with composure. "Just on unfamiliar territory."

His sudden smile, she thought, matched his voice, warm, appreciative, and with a hint of tenderness.

"Well answered," he had said, one hand sketching a mocking salute to her, and immediately turned away.

"And what were you thinking of, then?" Blanche asked, aware that her remark had, if not eliciting a satisfactory answer, set off a train of thought which the child had no right to keep to herself.

Lou, who had turned back to the wedding dress, and stood fingering its soft folds with an absent but appreciative touch, moved slowly round to face her cousin.

"Nothing that matters," she said. "Cousin Blanche, are the stories true?"

"What stories?"

"That Piers is paying your debts in exchange for Melissa?"

Blanche gave an imperceptible shug and her smile was indulgent and faintly bitter.

"Quite true, though you make it sound rather fustian melodrama," she replied. "We're broke, as I told you, Piers wants a wife, and all in all, the arrangement is very suitable. If you're thinking of high romance, my poor child, that's hardly Piers' conception of marriage. He's sown his wild oats and needs to settle down and found a family."

"And Melissa – doesn't she want more? Doesn't she want – "

Blanche frowned, looking at the girl with faint dislike.

"You sound rather impertinently censorious, Lou," she observed. "If you're thinking of that old affair, Melissa was scarcely serious about a penniless young actor who turned her head for a time."

Lou returned her cousin's look with slight bewilderment. She had not meant to be either impertinent or prying. She had not known Melissa well enough to be conversant with her love affairs, and she was only concerned with the present.

"Was there someone else, then?" she asked a little

timidly, and saw from her cousin's uneasy expression that she had touched on a sore subject

"My dear child, there had been dozens," Blanche replied impatiently. "Melissa is a beautiful girl, though I do say it myself."

"Then why worry?" Lou asked cheerfully, well aware of Melissa's attractions and only wishing to be helpful, but she became conscious at once of the dislike in her cousin's regard and wished she had not spoken. There was, she realised, suddenly, still some nagging worry at the back of Cousin Blanche's mind, despite the fact that her debts were paid and this lavish wedding would cost her nothing.

"Why should I worry?" Blanche said with a hard little edge to her voice. "Really, Lou, for a little girl who has been fortunate enough to participate in a world outside her own, you take rather much upon yourself, don't you think? Now, there are plenty of chores still to be done, so stop mooning over Melissa's wedding dress and come and make yourself useful. By the same token, don't, please, inflict Piers with your half-fledged views on the situation."

"I wouldn't," Lou replied, with a last, yearning look at the bridal gown which had become ghostly and mysterious in the failing daylight, "dream of discussing anything so personal with Piers – neither would he listen if I did."

"Naturally. Well, I'm glad that you're sensible enough to realize that for him you would scarcely count, even if you have rather fallen for him. Now, my dear, let's go downstairs and you can get on with listing the wedding presents. You'd better write out a few letters of thanks too – Melissa can just sign any but the most important." Blanche went out of the room and Lou followed her tall, graceful figure down the stairs, thinking how well the house's elegance suited her. It was a house hired for a few weeks, she knew, and the decor had been designed for someone else, but Cousin Blanche and her daughter, and their many acquaintances, would blend with the background of any fashionable London mansion and not care that none of them was a home.

As they crossed the hall, Melissa slid in at the front door and stood for a moment against it with the air of a truant who had been caught.

"Where have you been?" her mother demanded sharply, and to Lou there was an unwarranted anxiety in the question, just as there was a needless touch of defiance in Melissa's reply.

"Shopping, naturally," she retorted. "There are still a hundred and one things to remember. I returned the mink stole, incidentally, and exchanged it for a little jacket – red fox is in again, did you know?"

"Yes, I know. Rather double the cost of the stole, though, I imagine."

"Of course, but the sky's the limit, isn't it?"

"If you say so. Does Piers know he's to be responsible for your trousseau as well as our debts?"

"I haven't asked him. Still, darling, you're arranging all the sordid details of this business, aren't you?"

"Within reason. You haven't told me where you've been."

"*Shopping*, precious," Melissa said, her blue eyes wide and disingenuous. "We're shocking poor Lou, you know, with all this blatant talk of money. She's been brought up to believe that the trousseau and the wedding breakfast are matters for the bride's family, haven't you, Lou?"

Her cousin, Lou suspected, was deliberately proffering a red herring for her mother's distraction, but all the same she was aware that Melissa could never resist her little dig at what she termed *bourgeois* standards.

"I've never thought about it, not having been a prospective bride," Lou replied, and her cousin pulled a small grimace.

13

"Put in my place, you see," she said to her mother, "or could it be that my youngest bridesmaid is a tiny mite envious? Blanche darling, I'm dead to the world. Is Piers really coming tonight? Could I go to bed with a headache, do you suppose?"

Mother and daughter wandered together across the hall, tall and slim and coldly beautiful, their golden heads identical, thanks to an excellent but unimaginative hairdresser, their clothes differing hardly at all in design and elegance. Lou watched them, feeling gauche and alien. If they thought of her at all, they labelled her dull and ingenuous, she knew, the little cousin to whom one threw careless crumbs when she might prove useful, but whose feelings and opinions mattered nothing at all. Well, thought Lou, as the drawing-room door closed behind them, shutting her out, why should she care? She had been snatched up into a kind of fairy tale, thanks to the bridesmaid who had developed mumps, and if she did not altogether like what she found in this utterly foreign way of life, she could marvel and admire and store up the colour and the strangeness against the drab monotony of the office to which she would eventually return.

Each day Lou awakened to the small luxury of early morning tea, curtains drawn back by a maid, and all the unfamiliar attentions which she herself had never known but which for the Chaileys were presumably commonplace. Sometimes Melissa would come and share the tea, sitting on the bed while she smoked her endless cigarettes, lovely even in the cold early light.

There had never been any opportunity for the two girls to become intimate, neither, thought Lou, would Melissa have shown much interest in the rather dull little cousin who could not be expected to share in her own conception of what constituted a good time, but Lou had admired and been humble at so much careless perfection. Watching

Melissa now, and listening to accounts of parties, admirers, and the latest fashions, Lou sometimes wondered if her cousin merely wanted to impress or whether there was something on her mind which she wished to unload on to someone who was outside her usual run of intimates. If this last were true, Melissa certainly never got around to unburdening herself, and indeed, thought Lou, what could possibly be amiss in such an advantageous marriage to a man who, for so long, had been a prize just out of reach? She said as much on one occasion and was abashed by her cousin's rather cynical response.

"Oh, yes, he's a catch all right," she replied. "Blanche played her cards very well – all the same, she would find herself in the soup if I ratted, wouldn't she?"

"Ratted? You mean if you found you didn't want to marry him, after all? But surely – "

"Surely my happiness would come first with my mother, you were going to say, weren't you? Well, darling, the financial angle might be a bit tricky, mightn't it?"

"I wasn't going to say that, as it happens," Lou replied. "I'd meant surely you couldn't have any doubts now."

"Oh, I see. You think rather well of Piers, don't you? Blanche said you'd fallen for him."

"Cousin Blanche sees a lot in her imagination," Lou retorted sharply, and Melissa raised her eyebrows.

"Blanche doesn't imagine the obvious," she said with faint malice. "You wouldn't be the first to cherish an unrequited crush for our very eligible Mr. Merrick. He's been a hard enough fish to land in all conscience."

"That's horrid, coming from you," Lou said, frowning with distaste, and her cousin regarded her with amusement.

"In bad taste, you think?" Melissa countered with a slight drawl. "You're probably right; still and all – "

"Melissa – " Lou said tentatively as her cousin broke off, "if you *have* doubts – well, what did you mean when you said Cousin Blanche would find herself in the soup if you ratted?"

Melissa lit another cigarette and inhaled too quickly, making her cough.

"You must know the financial set-up by now, my dear. The other bridesmaids will scarcely have been very reticent," she observed coolly, and Lou moved uneasily in the bed. The bridesmaids, and Cousin Blanche herself, as far as that went, had been devastatingly frank; all the same –

"But Piers – " she began stubbornly. "He must be – he must be very much in love with you to – bargain, if that's what it comes to."

"You put it very tactfully, darling Lou, but Piers' emotions have remained undisturbed for years, I should imagine. Having sown his wild oats, as the saying is, he feels the need for settling down, and what better choice could he have than the daughter of the woman who should have been his stepmother?"

"Righting an old wrong, you mean?"

"Hardly that corny old chestnut! Getting his own back, more likely. He knows very well what a bitter pill it was to Blanche that she didn't wait long enough for that inheritance to come along. He was devoted to his father, you know, and had quite a thing about Blanche too, I believe. Why do you look so startled, Lou – or are you merely disapproving?"

"Not dis-disapproving," Lou stammered. "I just don't understand."

"No, you probably wouldn't – I'm not sure I do myself. There must be a streak of the romantic in Piers all mixed up with cocking snooks at Blanche – or maybe Blanche is just good at emotional blackmail. What do you think?"

Lou privately thought that the slightly alarming Piers Merrick kept his romantic streak well hidden, if indeed he

16

possessed one, neither had he appeared to her as a man to be swayed by blackmail, emotional or otherwise, but Melissa's approach to her coming marriage disturbed her rather more than the unknown sensibilities of the bridegroom.

"It's not my concern, is it?" she said at last. "Only – "

"Only what? The world well lost for love, you're thinking? But I like my love well gilded, darling, the fabulous wedding, the equally fashionable honeymoon, and after that – "

"After that," said Lou with unaccustomed asperity, "life on a small island with both of you cut down to size."

Her cousin looked at her with passing surprise.

"How very perceptive of you, darling," she observed, "But you don't imagine, do you, that I'm prepared to cut myself off from civilization on Piers' impossible island?"

"I understand the island is very much part of his background between travels."

"A fad – a gimmick. Who but Piers could afford, anyway, to buy an island off the Cornish coast, much less staff it and play king of the castle when the mood takes him? Oh, no, my child, once we're safely married Piers will sell his island and buy one of those so-called stately homes within reasonable distance of town. That and the London flat and the moor he rents each year for the grouse season will do very nicely for preventing us both from getting bored with each other."

Lou was used by now to her cousin's quite understandable little bursts of showing off, but she had, all at once, a sense of foreboding. Piers Merrick, she thought, was not the type of man to relinquish a cherished project for the sake of a pretty face ...

"The island is more than a gimmick. It's a refuge," she said.

"How should you know? He's like all rich men who can

indulge an expensive whim – crazy about it until it bores him."

"I think the island is more than that – a place of escape, a sort of touchstone."

"What nonsense you talk, impressionable Cousin Louise, but islands are romantic, of course – in theory. Has Piers been boring you with a lot of rubbish?"

"He hardly notices me," Lou replied gently, but remembering with an unreasoning pang of guilt the occasion of a dance she had attended with Melissa and the other bridesmaids whose escorts politely ignored her. Piers had suddenly plucked her from the little gilt chair where she sat against the wall, and without requesting a dance, had whirled her on to the floor. They had danced in complete silence, and she, aware that although he danced beautifully she was as good, abandoned herself wholeheartedly to the pleasure of the moment.

"*Well ...*" he had said when the music stopped, "you do surprise me, Cinderella."

"Do I? But Cinderella went to the ball, too."

"So she did – and captivated Prince Charming. You're like thistledown, Lou, or is that just a cliché?"

"I wouldn't know. I haven't many social graces."

"Haven't you?" His rather disillusioned eyes were suddenly bright with amusement. "But I think you're flirting with me – which is one of the graces."

She had stopped dead then in the middle of the dance floor as the music started again, and looked up at him in horrified confusion.

"I wouldn't dream ... I wouldn't dare ..." she stammered, and he gave a short snort of laughter as he swept her back into his arms.

"No, I don't believe you would at that," he said, and again danced in silence, giving her an impatient little shake as she missed a step because she was nervous.

They waltzed to quick, Viennese music, and after a

while, couples began to leave the floor and stood around to watch, and in the end she and Piers were left dancing alone and the evening became a dream. Cinderella, he had called her, not for the first time, and as they waltzed alone in the beam of a spotlight, she seemed caught up in a dream sequence which had no substance or reality.

There had been a small burst of applause when the music stopped and she had become aware of Cousin Blanche's look of displeasure and Melissa's amused expression of surprise. How had she known, then, that Piers' island was important to him, that it was a refuge, an escape from the life society had thrust upon him? But she had known, without a word on the subject exchanged.

"He hardly notices me," she had answered her cousin, and, of course, it was true; neither had he in his subsequent visits to the house, interrupting for a brief time the bustle and nervous tension of preparations for a big society wedding, neither did he, if it came to that, evince much impatience at his disturbed *tête-à-têtes* with his bride. Only Cousin Blanche, as the busy days flew by, seemed to become more on edge, snapping at Melissa whose absences on shopping expeditions, growing longer, seemed to worry her, snapping, too, at Lou who might be considered fair game for a display of temperament usually associated with the bride.

"Am I exceptionally stupid?" Lou asked of Jill, or Jane or Caroline, the other bridesmaids, who all looked much alike to her, and had clearly thought her of no account from the very beginning.

"No, darling, you're just a natural butt," Jill or Jane or Caroline answered, renewing her make-up with a practised hand. "Why do you run when you're whistled for? The bridemaids are only a decorative appendage to the bride."

Yes, in your case, Lou thought with rancour, but she was the poor relation, raised to the status of decorative appendage, it was true, but expected to work for the privilege.

"Cousin Blanche seems edgy – it's difficult to please," she said aloud.

"Your Cousin Blanche is just plain scared that there'll be a hitch at the last minute, darling. Melissa is causing anxiety."

"Melissa? But she seems calmer than anyone."

"Very likely she has her reasons. All the same, dear Cousin Blanche would be nicely in the soup, from all accounts, if anything went wrong. Piers made a very handsome settlement, you know, and that's already gone down the drain."

"Well," said Lou prosaically, firmly crushing down her own distaste for such blatant speculations, "what should go wrong? In a week they'll be married, and Melissa is scarcely likely to throw away a brilliant match at the last moment."

"No, I don't think so either, but they say history repeats itself."

"Cousin Blanche throwing over Piers' father, you mean?"

"Well, yes, but that was quite different, of course. Piers' father was a comparatively poor man then, and dear Blanche thought she knew which side her bread was buttered. I'm sure Melissa does, too."

"Yes . . . yes, I expect so," Lou replied absently, chiding herself for a sense of disappointment which she had learnt by now was old-fashioned and impracticable. The world was no longer well lost for love, and if one could know on which side one's bread was buttered, so much the better for all concerned.

"Darling, are you a little bit impressed with the gossip writers' dark hints about Piers?" Jill or Jane or Caroline enquired with idle curiosity.

"I don't read the gossip columns," Lou replied, fearing she sounded prim, and added with innocent enquiry, "What dark hints?"

"Oh, the usual. A modern rake, a young man given to extravagant whims, a young man who has lived his life and been pursued unavailingly – not that Piers is so young at that – he must be well on in the thirties. That wouldn't worry me, though, he's quite a dish, don't you think? And imagine all that gorgeous lolly?"

"A dish?" Lou knew, of course, what that meant, but the social insincerities of the age jarred her. *God bless*, they said, without stopping to think. *Take care of yourself*, they said, not really minding. A blessing came, perhaps, as no harm to anyone, but who would take care of you if you didn't do that for yourself? It was all so glib.

The bridesmaid whose name she could never remember was looking at her with resignation.

"An attraction, a prize, a feather worth having in one's cap," she said. "Things do have to be explained to you in words of one syllable, don't they, sweetie? We've all thought he made your girlish heart flutter a little."

"Have you? Then that was rather foolish," Lou replied coldly. "Because I haven't had the same chances in life as the rest of you there's no reason – no reason at all why – "

"For heaven's sake!" exclaimed the first or second or third bridesmaid in amazement, as Lou rushed suddenly from the room.

The last week drew to its hectic close, and Lou, despite the endless chores which fell to her lot and the increasing hysteria which seemed to be mounting in the people surrounding her, knew sharp regret that these brief weeks of extravagance were coming to an end. They had been a glimpse of storybook existence, a period of colour and excitement that would be remembered with gratitude when her own humdrum life was resumed and the office and the digs she shared with more ordinary mortals would bring her down to earth again. No matter that the house and servants were hired for the occasion, that Cousin Blanche's extravagant mode of living was no more than a whistling in the dark, no matter, again, that Melissa's romance, such a nine days' wonder, was no more than a union of mutual convenience with, from Blanche Chailey's point of view, a great deal of money at stake. It was still all a modern fairy tale, a dream-like, insubstantial snippet of life only gleaned at second hand, a life, when all was said and done, that would be very hard for the humble to live up to.

Here they were at last on the eve of the wedding, with rain pouring down unkindly from the November sky with no promise of relenting for the morrow. The bridesmaids were all assembled for a final fitting of their dresses, the door bell rang incessantly, also the telephone, the vast double drawing-room was already cleared for the reception and in the hands of the caterers, and Blanche moved restlessly from one room to another, countermanding orders, snapping at all and sundry, bewailing the weather and her daughter's unaccountable absence alike.

"Where is Melissa?" she demanded for the twentieth time. "She knows there's a final rehearsal this afternoon, and anyway she should be resting."

"She went out early. I think she was going to church," Lou said, trying to sound soothing, but her cousin merely laughed derisively.

"If she told you that, Lou, then she thinks you're a bigger fool than I took you for," she retorted, but Lou's widely spaced eyes simply grew wider in genuine puzzlement.

"I don't understand. It seemed to me very natural that Melissa should wish to go to church alone," she said gently, but Cousin Blanche favoured her with a look of impatience which bordered on dislike.

"I daresay it does," she snapped. "But to my knowledge Melissa has never before shown desire to beg a blessing on any of her projects. Why should she now?"

"Marriage is a little different. One would want to ask

a blessing for that, I think," Lou replied gravely, then looked round quickly for the familiar expressions of surprise or ridicule on the faces of the bridesmaids, but they were all too busy admiring themselves to pay her attention, even if they had heard her.

Cousin Blanche had already turned away to restore order with a few pungent sentences, and Lou crossed to one of the mirrors to study her own reflection in comparative peace. The dresses were charming, she thought, discovering with faint wonder what the cunningly cut moss green velvet sheath did for herself. She was the youngest, and by far the most slender of all the bridesmaids, and the dress seemed fashioned, she thought, with herself in mind. The image in the mirror seemed for a moment that of a stranger. The colour was complementary to her own muted tones, and the soft, slender lines kind to her sharp young bones. I look almost pretty, she thought with pleasure, then her cousin's voice observed behind her:

"For heaven's sake, Lou, why won't you let them do something about your hair? You'll be the only one with a head not properly dressed. I can still get an appointment for you," Blanche snapped.

"No, no, madame, Mademoiselle is quite right!" the head fitter's voice broke in, and she began giving deft twitches to the shoulders and long tight sleeves, smiling over Lou's head as she did so. "The simplicity is right for the gown, that straight, soft fall of hair, the little fringe – it is right and charming. A wood nymph, perhaps, would you say?"

"I would say you're putting a lot of silly nonsense into the child's head," Blanche replied tartly. "Wood nymph, indeed! Well, she'll scarcely be noticed amongst the others, so I don't suppose it matters."

When she was out of hearing the fitter whispered angrily:

"Do not heed her, mademoiselle. She is annoyed because she knows that you alone can wear this gown with grace."

"Oh, I don't think so," Lou replied with honest surprise. "Anyway I shall never wear it again, I don't suppose. It would be too grand for the sort of life I lead."

"What a pity," the woman remarked, but the look she gave Lou was suddenly curious and faintly ironic, and Lou realized in a moment of embarrassment that Cousin Blanche had not fooled her at all. The cost of the wedding and the fabulous trousseau might impress the credulous, but it was evidently common knowledge that the wealthy bridegroom would have to meet the bills.

"Thank you," Lou said, moving quickly away, feeling suddenly ashamed. Cousin Blanche, if she could not afford it, did not have to put on such a reckless display of extravagance, nor did her daughter have to acquiesce so complacently, and where, indeed, *was* Melissa on a rainy afternoon when she should have been fitting her wedding dress? The final rehearsal was to be a full dress affair at home, so that trains and unfamiliar trappings could be manoeuvred without disaster on the day and the picture as a whole scrutinized and made perfect. Very soon the bridegroom would arrive; neither he nor Melissa or her mother apparently attached any importance to the old superstition that it was unlucky for the groom to see the wedding dress before the ceremony.

Cousin Blanche was beginning to panic, and even the waiting bridesmaids started whispering and giggling among themselves. The head fitter was complaining with rising indignation that there would not be enough time to dress the bride and be ready for the rehearsal and her apprentices could not spend all the afternoon in idleness when there might be last-minute alterations to be made.

"Be quiet!" snapped Blanche, and a maid came into the room at that moment and handed her a letter.

"Come by hand," she vouchsafed laconically. "There's

no answer."

There was nothing in the trivial interruption to cause alarm, but Lou watched while her cousin slit the envelope and felt suddenly afraid. Even the chattering bridesmaids fell silent as if disquiet had touched them, too, and Blanche herself froze into rigidity as she read the contents of the note.

"Madame ..." the head fitter murmured, sensing disaster, but when Blanche spoke her voice was like ice, and her face looked suddenly old.

"Will you all go, please? You won't be required here any longer," she said.

"But the wedding gown?"

"The wedding dress will have to wait. My daughter's been – delayed."

"Cousin Blanche ..." Lou said as the door closed softly behind the fitter and her assistants, then Blanche suddenly went to pieces.

"She's gone!" she screamed on a rising note of hysteria. "Melissa has done this to me ... run off with that good-for-nothing young charmer I'd thought safely forgotten, just because of a tiff with Piers ... love is all that counts, she says. Love! As if such nonsense mattered with the world at your feet and a fortune already spent in advance. Don't stand there like a lot of gaping dummies – there'll be no wedding so you might as well all go home –"

"Cousin Blanche!" Lou's young voice was sharp with distress and she made an instinctive movement towards the older woman, then drew back, embarrassed and dismayed. It was terrible to witness such a cracking of that hitherto hard, cold façade; it was hurtful to interpret the avid expressions on the pretty faces of the girls enjoying her humiliation.

Jane – or perhaps it was Caroline – said in an audible whisper:

"History repeating itself with a vengeance! Who's going

25

to tell the high and mighty bridegroom he's been left at the altar?''

Who, indeed? thought Lou distractedly, and as if on cue, Piers walked unannounced into the room.

CHAPTER TWO

He stood there for a moment surveying them all with a quizzical expression. The bridesmaids had instinctively ranged themselves in a line against the wall and his eyes travelled slowly over them each in turn.

"Very charming," he observed. "And where's the bride – or am I late?"

No one answered him, and his attention turned to Blanche. She had control of herself now, shocked into immobility by his sudden appearance, but her face was drawn beneath the careful mask of make-up and she caught her breath on the last remaining note of hysteria.

"Is anything amiss?" Piers enquired politely, and Lou had the uncomfortable impression that not only was he instantly warned of disaster but was in some measure enjoying himself.

"Well, is nobody going to explain why you all look at me as if I were the spectre at the feast!" he continued as nobody spoke. "You, Cinderella – you're usually the one given the unpleasant jobs. Won't you break it to me gently? Have I been left at the altar like my father before me?"

His eyes coming to rest on Lou's distressed face were hard and suddenly without amusement and there was an imperceptible tightening at the corners of his mouth. He was not enjoying himself, after all, thought Lou, wondering why she should have imagined he was, and because someone had to tell him and Cousin Blanche was coming to no one's rescue she said with a baldness that inexperience could not soften:

"Yes, you have, I'm afraid. Melissa's run away with someone else."

The little pause that followed seemed to her like a

moment suspended in time. The bridesmaids became frozen into a waiting silence. Blanche made a small, nervous gesture and then was still, and Lou herself searched out a corner of the room where she could merge into obscurity.

Piers' lean, dark face showed little change. He surveyed them all with an expression which suggested that someone might have committed in impertinence.

"Has she, indeed? Well now, Blanche, what do you propose to do about that?" He was extremely cool, extremely unsurprised, but Lou realized, if the others did not, that he was also dangerously angry.

"What do you expect me to do, my dear Piers?" Blanche, whose only course lay in brazening things out, was momentarily deceived by his manner. "The girl, of course, must be slightly unhinged, but as I don't know where she is at the moment, I can't do much about getting her back. You'd better read her note." She handed over the letter and he stood reading it in silence, then folded it carefully and handed it back.

"Love is all that counts," he quoted reflectively. "Dear me, I wouldn't have thought that sort of cliché would have come from Melissa. Well now, Blanche, I repeat — what are you going to do?"

"And I've told you there's nothing I can do. We will have to postpone the marriage, of course. I'll think up something for the press."

"Postpone it?"

"Well, there's hardly time between now and tomorrow to learn her whereabouts and get her brought back."

"And if I don't choose to postpone it?"

"You scarcely have much choice."

"But you, my dear Blanche, have less. We made a bargain, you and I, with your daughter a very willing hostage. Are you able to return my money?" he said very gently, and at last Blanche began to look afraid.

"You know very well that's impossible, but I, no more

28

than you, expected to be let down at the last moment."

"Didn't you? But your charming daughter is only following your example, after all."

"That was very different. You're a rich man, Piers, you can afford to be generous."

His eyes suddenly narrowed. "Yes, I'm a rich man, and for that reason I don't choose to be made a laughing stock of. I can make you bankrupt, my dear, and the scandal won't be pleasant. I was to foot the bills for the wedding and trousseau too, wasn't I – or did you imagine I didn't know I was being milked?"

The bridesmaids had drawn together in little groups, whispering among themselves. Blanche glanced at their worldly-wise faces, well aware that the scandal would be all over London by nightfall, and anxious creditors probably on the doorstep by morning.

"You girls had better go and change," she said sharply. "And please don't leave until I've had a word with you all."

"Let them stay," Piers said. "You won't muzzle their gossiping little tongues once they get home, and your financial excesses are pretty well known anyway."

"Do you want to humiliate me by making me beg for generosity in front of them?" Blanche asked, and unwonted tears filled her eyes.

He was silent for a moment, remembering her as she had seemed to him as a small boy, beautiful, elegant and sweet-smelling, his ideal of the mother he could not remember.

"Oh, dear me, no, that would be most embarrassing for everyone," he answered, and now the voice which had beguiled the impressionable Lou before ever they met was light and casual. "There's no real problem for you, Blanche. The marriage will proceed."

She closed her eyes for a moment, faint with relief.

"I knew you'd be reasonable, Piers," she said. "It won't mean a long postponement. I'll hire detectives. I'll have her brought back, eating humble pie. Melissa's very sensible, really – she'll soon find out her mistake."

"But that will be a little late, won't it? I don't think I would care for a bride who had anticipated her wedding night with someone else." There was a chill in his voice, which should have warned her.

"But there's no other way out."

"Oh, I think there is. You must find me a substitute, that's all."

She stared at him incredulously.

"Are you mad?" she asked, and he ran an absent hand over his chin as if to satisfy himself that his morning shave had been entirely satisfactory.

"I don't think so," he replied. "My chief need was a wife, if you remember, and for old times' sake, your daughter seemed a suitable choice, but since she's had other ideas, it makes little difference."

"Little difference? What on earth do you mean?"

He stood there, quite at ease now, his hands thrust in his trouser pockets, his dark head tilted back a little, surveying them all through half-closed eyes, and Lou, watching him, remembered the gossip and the colourful stories which had seemed to follow in the wake of the name of Merrick. Money and self-assurance, she supposed, could give one this strange right to autocracy.

"I mean quite simply that I don't intend to be made a fool of," he said then. "Thanks to you there has been too much publicity about this affair, so why not a bit more? I refuse to be the subject of ridicule by the cancellation of tomorrow's programme, so find me another bride."

"Really, Piers, you're carrying this Rajah complex a little far, don't you think?"

"You must be mistaken in the complex – I have no harem," he replied. "And with all due modesty I might add that I'm considered quite a catch in the matrimonial market, so where's your difficulty?"

"You're insufferable!" Blanche exclaimed, with her first genuine burst of feeling, and he gave her a quick, wholly charming smile.

"I am, aren't I?" he agreed. "Still, I have my pride like anyone else, and tomorrow's ceremony goes on — so what?"

"So what — as you say?" Blanche echoed, suddenly sitting down on the nearest chair. "I don't think I feel very well. Does it mean so little to you, Piers, to replace Melissa with a stranger at the eleventh hour?"

He looked down at her, smiling again that quick charming smile which Lou was beginning to think hid a great deal which he did not care to reveal. The whole fantastic interview was so bizarre that she had begun to regard it as a natural culmination to the past unreal weeks.

"Well, now, that's rather a leading question, don't you think?" he replied. "You and I both know that this marriage was a matter of expediency rather than a starry-eyed romance. Melissa has, of course, proved me wrong in that respect, but as far as I'm concerned, one bride is as good as another, providing she takes to me kindly. Now here you have a bevy of charming young girls, all hoping for husbands in due course. One of them might oblige, wouldn't you think?"

The goggling bridesmaids, after the first incredulous gasp, entered into the spirit of the thing with a will, clustering round him, laughing and preening.

"You see," he said, throwing a glance at Blanche that was at once humorous and disillusioned. He considered them all for a moment with weary attention, then suddenly wheeled round on the youngest bridesmaid, standing apart and clearly not enjoying the situation.

"And what about you, Cinderella?" he asked with mocking deliberation. "You don't, I notice, seem anxious to fill the shoes of the defaulting bride."

Lou stood there, licking her dry lips, unsure still if he

were jesting or not, and acutely embarrassed at being singled out for his attention.

"I don't take you seriously, which is just as well," she replied, and her eyes looked suddenly enormous in her pale, slightly scandalized face.

"Why is it just as well? Would you have me?" he said, and watched the betraying colour tinge her skin with a fleeting suggestion of beauty.

"I – I don't care for these sort of jokes, and – and marriage is a serious business," she stammered, and for a moment his face wore that strange touch of tenderness which she had glimpsed once or twice before.

"Yes, it is, and I'm quite serious, too," he said with sudden gentleness. "You would suit very well, I'm beginning to think, Cousin Lou, and we still keep it in the family, which should please your cousin Blanche. Will you have me?"

They were all looking at her, the bridesmaids in varying degrees of disgust and astonishment, Cousin Blanche with her face already settling into its habitual fashionable mask now that a compromise had been reached, and Piers, the dark, arrogant stranger who believed he had only to whistle up a bride and she would come running; a monstrous suggestion, a monstrous situation!

"C-certainly not!" Lou replied in outraged tones and, bursting into tears, fled from the room.

After that nothing to Lou had been sane or real. Cousin Blanche's pleadings had been desperate and undignified, the bridesmaids' comments unflattering, if well-intentioned, and nobody seemed to stop talking, arguing, or quarrelling.

"You must be mad to throw away such an opportunity," Cousin Blanche had said, finally getting rid of the bridesmaids who were only adding to the confusion. "Here are you, a little nobody, refusing the chance of a lifetime for the sake of some romantic scruple, to say nothing of repaying my own kindness with ingratitude. I wanted him for Melissa, that's true, but at least I can accept a change of heart with a good grace."

"Because," Lou retorted, driven to honesty, "you think he would make you bankrupt, otherwise."

"I don't think, I know," Blanche snapped. "Don't imagine in your trusting innocence that Piers wouldn't carry out his threat if he fails to get what he wants. He has old scores to pay off, and he's a proud man."

"He doesn't want me. He's hardly ever noticed me."

"I'm not so sure. That time you danced . . . the way he sometimes teased you . . . he was never in love with Melissa, you know. They simply suited for the moment."

"I don't suppose he's ever loved anyone."

"Very likely not, but you, Lou – you lost your heart to him a little, so marriage shouldn't be too difficult . . ."

"No . . . no . . . *no!*" repeated Lou with infuriating stubbornness, and her cousin, for the moment, gave up.

"You'd better go and change your dress," she said coldly. "Heaven knows how it's going to get paid for now anyway."

Lou rose obediently and started across the hall already dim and shadowy in the failing light. It must be late afternoon, she supposed, and the house seemed suddenly very quiet after the ceaseless rise and fall of feminine voices. The caterers had gone, but the drawing-room doors stood open, and she peeped inside to gaze disconsolately on the lavish preparations for the reception. Tears of regret for the ignominious ending to Cousin Blanche's bright schemes sprang to her eyes as she looked. The scent of the hothouse flowers, which, alone, must have cost a fortune, was already overpowering, and there was such a predominating note of white, ghostly and rather funereal, in the shadows that Lou shivered.

"It's like a wake, not a wedding," she said aloud.

"Yes, it is rather," Piers' voice observed unexpectedly

behind her, and two firm hands came to rest lightly on her shoulders.

She turned swiftly round to face him, taken utterly by surprise.

"I thought you'd gone long ago," she said.

"I'm still waiting for my answer," he replied, one finger touching with gentle curiosity a tear that still clung to her lashes. "Has Blanche been bullying you?"

"No, not really – and you had my answer."

"But I'd hoped you weren't serious."

"Why? Because no girl has ever turned you down before?"

He smiled with surprised amusement at this unexpected flash of bravado, and gave her a little shake.

"You know nothing about my much publicized love-life," he said with mock severity.

"Only what I read in the gossip columns."

"Exactly. And think what a whale of a ball the gossip writers are going to have after tomorrow if you insist on remaining stubborn."

"I don't see," Lou replied wearily, "that it will make much difference. They'd be pop-eyed anyway with a change of bride."

"Quite true, but that's an entirely different kettle of fish; no resurrected scandals for poor Cousin Blanche, no hungry creditors on the doorstep, only a last-minute conjuring tricks to whet the public's appetite. It's a scoop handed out on a plate to any ambitious reporter."

"What should I care about the public's appetite? Besides – "

"Like me, my child, damn all! Besides what?"

"You can't get married to somebody else at a moment's notice. It wouldn't be legal."

"Are you weakening? There's such a thing as a special licence – all perfectly legal."

"Oh! How long – "

34

" – would it take? I've already done it, while you women were wrangling in the other room."

If he had not held her with sudden firmness she would have slipped away from his hands.

"*You* – you were so sure that I couldn't resist such a prize that you – oh, you're quite impossible!" she cried, but her struggling ceased as his finger traced another tear along her lashes.

"I'm not such a prize, dear Lou," he said with humility. "Don't think that because I'm rich and what the scandal sheets have termed a catch, I don't know my own short-comings. I really haven't asked for half the wild surmises that have been flying around, you know."

"No, I don't suppose you have," she said, wondering if he had talked to Melissa like this. But Melissa would not have cared. Melissa only wanted a share in the publicity, no matter how untrue it was, and even she, in the end, had settled for her heart's dictates.

"Well?" he said.

"Well what?"

"You know very well. Look, Lou, I admit I was riled, possibly beyond reason, at this rather salutory slap in the face, and I admit that I had every intention of making your dear Cousin Blanche pay, not only for getting every cent out of me she could, but for her treatment of my father. Do you think that unreasonable?"

"I don't know. Does one bear grudges so far back?"

He looked suddenly weary with the old look of dis-illusionment.

"It was hardly a grudge in quite that sense," he said. "I suppose what one loses suddenly as a child can colour one's life. I thought Blanche was wonderful, you see. I had never known my own mother, and Blanche – well, she naturally made much of me, I suppose, since she was going to marry my father."

There was a little silence. The shadows had deepened

even as they talked, and outside the rain still beat relent-lessly down. Cousin Blanche, thought Lou inconsequentially, must have known that Piers was waiting to plead his own cause.

"Yes . . . I see . . ." Lou said, moved despite herself, but hardly aware of what it was she saw.

"You're very tired, aren't you?" Piers said, feeling the sudden slackness in her limbs. "Don't worry about these things any more. I would like you to know, though, that my ultimatum to your cousin wasn't entirely the piece of blackmail you all took it for."

"Then you won't – ?"

His face hardened at once. "Oh yes, I will, but that has nothing to do with you now."

"But it has. Cousin Blanche – well, I can't let her be ruined for the sake of – for the sake of – "

"For the sake of what? Your cousin might be more than temporarily embarrassed, as they say, but she wouldn't be ruined in the long run. Someone would come to the rescue, someone always has."

"I don't know what you're trying to tell me," Lou said.

"I'm trying to tell you that I want to marry you, my dear – that I think, if you are not averse to me, that you are, perhaps, what I need – or am I being high-and-mighty again? One never knows."

Lou had little fight left in her, and the tenderness was back in his face, the tenderness that matched the warmth of his voice which had first charmed her.

"No, you're not being high-and-mighty, Piers – what can I do?"

"Marry me. Oh, it won't be all beer and skittles in spite of my wealth, and I'm possibly too old for you, still – "

"Still – " echoed Lou, too tired for further argument, and Piers bent his head to kiss her. His lips, warm and unexpectedly tender on hers, were a benediction and her eyes flew open.

"That wasn't fair," she said.

"Not fair? But you are going to marry me – aren't you?"

"Yes . . ." she said on a note of surprise, and a little sigh of relief escaped her that the long struggle was over, that this stranger to whom she was suddenly pledged might have, after all, a strange, unexpected solace to give.

"Thank you," he said, releasing her. "Now I can leave. Till tomorrow, then, Lou, and – be of good heart. God bless!"

Tomorrow . . . Tomorrow had inevitably come, of course, but not before Lou was worn out with the many arrangements which immediately engulfed her. She must wear Melissa's wedding dress, Cousin Blanche ordained; there was no time to arrange anything else, and the two girls were much the same size. The fitters were recalled and Lou stood clad in the miraculous fairy-tale creation which had first captured her imagination, while the fitters pinned and snipped, deftly reducing and shortening, for although reasonably the same build, Lou was noticeably more slender and Melissa the taller of the two.

"Ah, mademoiselle, the gown is ravishing," the head fitter said, and Lou wondered what she was thinking at this extraordinary turn of events, but to Lou now, and possibly to the tired woman working stoically overtime, it no longer much mattered what anyone thought.

"You must take such of the trousseau as you may need, for you've nothing suitable yourself," Cousin Blanche said magnanimously, and Lou had looked at Melissa's exquisite wardrobe and acquiesced in anything that was suggested. Mink hung from the padded hangers, sleekly elegant coats and stoles and the fox jacket which only a few days ago Melissa had exchanged so recklessly.

"Not that," said Lou, remembering that it had been treble the cost of the stole and a rather mean extravagance in view of her subsequent behaviour.

"Now listen carefully, Lou . . ." Cousin Blanche said, it

37

seemed for the hundredth time. So many instructions, so many admonitions; so much to remember, so much to forget, such little time left to remain oneself. Already, she seemed to have taken on another personality, wearing Melissa's wedding dress, going away with Melissa's trousseau, and Melissa herself – where was she? Had she found happiness with the man she loved? Had she no regrets for the brilliant future she had thrown away? No one, thought Lou in the last numbed stages of exhaustion, had given a thought to Melissa. From her mother's point of view she had acted out of character and ruined a flawless scheme, and what happened to her now could scarcely concern anyone but herself.

"Poor Melissa . . ." Lou murmured as at long last she crept thankfully into her bed, already half asleep. "I hope she's happy . . . I hope she'll never know what she's missed . . ." But she was not thinking of the ease and luxury of the future as she fell asleep mourning a little for her cousin, but of that autocratic stranger with whom, had she wanted, Melissa could have found so much. . . .

At last it was over. Lou, treated for the first time in her life to the attention and consideration shown to someone of first importance, submitted docilely to all that was planned for her, and felt very little. It was not she, she thought, when she thought at all, who had suddenly become the hub of a fashionable occasion, but a dream self moving obediently through a day of make-believe. She had been stand-in for a bridesmaid, now she was stand-in for the bride, and none of it was real. She was aware of the crowds waiting at the church and the excited murmurs of astonishment and speculation as she began the long walk up the aisle.

The voices of the choir rose and fell in some unfamiliar anthem, the blur of faces on either side were unfamiliar, too, as was the subtle drag and pull of Melissa's miraculous wedding dress trailing behind her, and suddenly Lou was grateful for her shoes. Melissa's hand-made models of perfection had not fitted, and Lou had been obliged to wear her own well-worn and rather tarnished slippers. They were, she thought, a salutary reminder that underneath all the borrowed glory she was still little Lou Parsons, a girl who just for a day was deputising for another and who would in the end, like the Cinderella of the story, hear the chimes of midnight strike, turning the pomp and glitter back into pumpkins and white mice.

What absurd things one thinks of, she reflected, aware with surprise that the long procession up the aisle was nearly over, that the choir had stopped singing, and the dark stranger waiting at the altar rails had turned to meet her. For a moment reality pierced through the dream and she stopped dead. What, she wondered wildly, was she doing here? How had she allowed herself to become persuaded into such a farce? Then Piers smiled, that slightly twisted smile with its redeeming touch of tenderness, and she moved forward to stand beside him.

From then on she was back again in the dream. She listened to Piers making his responses firmly and clearly, and her own were no less clear; only when the ring was put on her finger did she falter, for it was too big and had plainly been meant for Melissa. Piers' smile was wryly amused as he slipped it on, and she wondered if already he was regretting that outrageous gesture to save his own pride. Only then did she fully realize what she had done; for better or worse, she was married to a man she scarcely knew, a man who had said so arrogantly: "I refuse to be made the subject of ridicule . . . so find me another bride." She, the unlikely puppet of his choosing, had allowed herself to be persuaded into madness, but not on account of her cousin's pleadings, but because he himself, waiting so unexpectedly for her answer, had with that strange flash of tenderness swept away her defences.

They were in the vestry now to sign the register, and for the last time Lou wrote her name, Louise Mary Parsons, and said goodbye to that other self. Cousin Blanche kissed her and so did several strangers; the bridegroom had not appeared to think it necessary, an omission which had already been avidly noted by some of the ladies present; then she was walking down the aisle on Piers' arm, conscious now of the craning necks and muted buzz of talk on either side. They came out into the daylight to a battery of cameras and reporters excitedly demanding a story, and Lou stood listening to the peal of bells, aware that yesterday's rain had begun again, that strange faces gazed at her from under a sea of umbrellas and wet gleamed on the cape of a mounted policeman clearing a way for them through the crowd. She had seen it all so many times on television newsreels, the wedding of the week, the wedding of the year, wondering what it felt like to be the bride, and now she played that role herself and felt nothing. Careful hands were lifting the yards of velvet after her into the car, and she saw with a sense of guilt that the hem was already splashed with mud; she clasped her hands nervously in her lap, the cuffs of white mink soft against her wrists, and as the car moved slowly away, Piers' hand closed over hers with sudden warmth.

"You came through that very nicely – very nicely indeed," he said. "Were you nervous?"

"No," she replied in all honesty. "You see, I didn't believe in any of it. It was just makebelieve."

One eyebrow shot up, giving his face a momentary look of distortion.

"Then you'll have to come down to earth, won't you? I can assure you I have no plans for a makebelieve marriage," he said, and whether it was intended as a threat or a warning, the remark embarrassed her.

"I didn't mean . . ." she began tentatively. "I – I realize that . . . I mean, I'm trying to say . . ."

"Well, what are you trying to say?"

"You don't make it very easy."

"You'll find, I'm afraid, my dear Lou, that I won't often make things easy for you. I'm not an easy person, so I'm told."

"I think you probably rather pride yourself on that," she replied unexpectedly. "When a person's spoilt and run after it doesn't become necessary to consider other people."

"Good grief, who'd have expected a set-down only a quarter of an hour after marriage!" he exclaimed with humour. "Do you think I'm spoilt?"

"I don't know you," she said, and as the car braked suddenly and skidded a little on the wet road, she found herself flung against his shoulder. He put an arm round her to steady her, at the same time brushing his lips against her cheek.

"You've sidetracked the original subject quite neatly, haven't you? I thought you were endeavouring to make it plain that you were fully prepared to accept the – er – more intimate responsibilities of marriage," he said, and when she did not immediately answer he gave a wry little smile. "You hadn't thought of that side, had you?" he added quite gently.

No, she hadn't thought. There had been no time since yesterday to reflect on more sober things in a world which had suddenly gone crazy.

"I don't suppose you'll find me up to your usual standards, but I can learn," she said, trying to sound both obliging and dignified, but fearing, when he laughed, that she had only succeeded in appearing absurd.

"And what do you suppose are my usual standards, as you so delicately put it?" he asked.

"Well, you like your women sophisticated – experienced – so they say."

"Do I? Then you'll make a wholesome change, won't you, Lou? Ah, here we are. Better brace yourself for this

41

reception, my poor child; there are going to be a lot of awkward questions asked."

There was, indeed, a great deal of polite and not so polite curiosity in the air, but as Lou knew scarcely any of the guests it was not too difficult to evade the more blatant remarks. Cousin Blanche, who herself was very skilled at dealing with impertinences, had obviously cooked up some sort of explanation to quell, if not silence, the gossipers, but the bridesmaids, as Piers had pointed out yesterday, could not be muzzled for ever, and would doubtless dine out on the true story for weeks to come.

The cake was cut, toasts were drunk, and somebody made a speech which, possibly by reason of the last-minute switch-over of brides, was not in the happiest vein. Piers replied with something of a bite and, very soon, Cousin Blanche was bustling Lou upstairs to change. It was high time, Blanche thought, to bring these proceedings to an end, before more embarrassing questions were put; only just now someone had asked where the honeymoon was to be spent, and that dazed-looking child had replied that she didn't know.

"Really, Lou!" Cousin Blanche said, as she shepherded the bride up the stairs. "You knew Melissa's plans perfectly well. Paris, Rome, Vienna, a short luxury tour of the great capitals of Europe. I'm beginning to think, though, it will all be wasted on you."

Lou thought so, too. Melissa she could well picture in the honeymoon suites of expensive hotels, dancing the night long, spending money, never allowing boredom to ruffle the seasoned dictates of her exacting bridegroom, and as she submitted to the experienced hands which stripped her of her wedding finery and dressed her again in one of the elegant suits from Melissa's trousseau, Lou experienced a moment's terror at the prospect of her immediate future. How would she, who had never been out of England, know how to comport herself in foreign countries? How,

42

above all, know in what way to meet the demands and expectations of a man who had already travelled the world over and could find nothing new?

She stood passively before a long mirror while the final touches were made, Melissa's fabulous mink coat slung carelessly about her shoulders, gloves and handbag put into her unresisting hands.

Somebody gave her the wedding bouquet, and she looked at it blankly. "What am I to do with it?" she asked.

"Throw it, of course," the head fitter smiled, amused.

"Throw it?"

"To the bridesmaids. Whoever catches it will be the next — surely you know?"

"Oh, yes, I'd forgotten." Lou surprised a brief flash of compassion, or it might only have been suppressed curiosity, in the woman's worldly eyes, and remembered how she had seemed to side with Lou when fitting the bridesmaids' dresses, and indeed, in respectful but firm fashion, put Cousin Blanche in her place.

"Thank you for all your help, and all your patience," Lou said shyly. "You must think — "

"I'm not paid to think, mademoiselle — or rather, I should say now, madame," the fitter replied repressively, then she suddenly smiled. "Go now, for they are waiting, and — good luck."

Good luck ... good luck ... thought Lou as she walked to the head of the stairs. She would need all the luck in the world to meet the new life waiting for her, to make a success of a marriage so haphazardly thrust upon her, to learn to love a bridegroom who had chosen her with such ill-considered impetuosity.

She dutifully flung her bouquet to the group of bridesmaids, but did not notice who caught it, then was aware of Piers at her elbow, pushing a way through the chattering throng. His long black sports convertible stood at the kerb, its hood up since it was raining, and, a little bemused by the banter and embraces from perfect strangers pleasantly mellowed by champagne, she clambered into the car rather awkwardly and felt her stocking run as she did so.

They were away with the noisy burst of acceleration that such a car and such a driver demanded, and Lou remembered that Piers' driving had alarmed her.

"Well?" he said, manoeuvring skilfully through the traffic.

"I've laddered my tights," she replied with childish inconsequence, and after that they drove in silence, leaving the busy thoroughfares behind for the wet mazes of the suburbs, and the suburbs in turn for the first beginnings of country. Lou had no idea whether they were heading north, south, east or west; they seemed enclosed in a nameless small world unrelated to anything familiar, and the windscreen wipers began to have a hypnotic effect on her.

"Where are we going?" she asked at last, because someone must break the uncomfortable silence, but he answered her indirectly

"It wasn't very quick of you to tell that gossiping old tabby that you didn't know where your honeymoon was to be spent," he observed, but she surprised him, as before, with an unexpected retort.

"Very likely, but since no one had seen fit to acquaint me I could hardly be expected to know," she replied.

"Yes, you have something there," he said quite mildly, then braked so violently to avoid a wool-gathering cyclist that she caught at and then held on to the padded arm-rest between them.

"Nervous?" he asked, sounding rather as if he would enjoy frightening her.

"Yes," she said, too honest to wish to impress him with false courage, and he immediately reduced their progress to a reasonable cruising speed and gently loosening the grip of her hand on the arm-rest, returned it to her lap.

"Relax," he said. "Do you drive, Lou?"

"No."

"One day I'll teach you."

"Not in this!"

"No, possibly not in this. A high-powered car, like a capricious woman, needs handling with understanding."

"What a very trite remark," observed Lou with surprise rather than with any wish to be pert, for she had not thought him obvious, and he brought the car to a sudden standstill by the side of the road with a squeal of tyres on the wet tarmac.

"For the youngest bridesmaid who, until now, has been kept firmly in the background, you have developed a rather disconcerting mind of your own, my dear," he said, and she realized that he was angry.

She drew a little away from him, aware that her expressions of opinion had possibly been only a form of whistling in the dark.

"I'm sorry," she said. "I didn't mean to be rude. You just surprised me."

"In what way?"

"Well – smart sayings like that. I shouldn't have thought – "

"Upon my soul, you've got a nerve!" he interrupted, frowning down upon her. "Did you think I was trying to impress you?"

"N-not exactly. I – I don't really know what to think any more. I still can't believe any of it."

He caught the first suggestion of tears in her voice and the irritable lines smoothed out in his face.

"You poor little thing, you're worn out, aren't you?" he said. "We've asked a lot of you, Blanche and I, but –will it help if I say I didn't choose at random?"

"Didn't you?" Her eyes were suspiciously bright and she sounded now as if she neither believed nor cared. "But you've hardly noticed me."

"More than you think. For a start, you of all those

45

twittering young women didn't chatter, neither did you fidget, and those are two good assets in a wife."

She was conscious of fidgeting now, and instinctively sat on her hands. He was, she supposed, only trying to rally her with not very serious nonsense, but all the same, in implying that the choice had been his with little fear of refusal he betrayed the fact that for him conquests had always been too easy. "Piers – " she began.

"Well?"

"Nothing," she retracted lamely. She was too tired and too muddled to put her intimate feelings into words, too confused, she realized now, even to know what they were.

"Are you, by any chance, getting cold feet about our wedding night?" he asked, the old ironical twist back in his voice.

"No," she said. "At least, that wasn't what I was thinking of."

"Weren't you, indeed? Well, remember what I told you coming back from the church. My plans don't include a makebelieve marriage. I wasn't sure if you quite understood."

"I understood perfectly," she replied gravely. "You – you won't find me ignorant. I've been taught the facts of life, you know."

For a moment she glimpsed that flash of tenderness in his smile.

"I'm glad to hear it. I wouldn't like you to find your Prince Charming had turned into an ogre – Cinderella," he said, and turned on the ignition.

The powerful roar of the engine sounded rather like an ogre's threat to eat you up, Lou thought, wondering for the first time what sort of lover he would make and whether he would be selfish or considerate, then the car leapt forward again. The late afternoon light had already deepened to twilight, and Lou ceased watching the speedometer needle reaching seventy, eighty, ninety and sank into an exhausted doze.

She must have slept, for when she next opened her eyes it was quite dark. The rain, she thought, must have stopped, for the twin wipers were at rest; she imagined she saw the first stars pricking through the sky, but it might only have been the lights of some distant village, or even the imaginings of her own desire for the breaking up of the darkness.

She slept again, this time leaning unconsciously against Piers' shoulder, then the piercing squeal of tyres woke her, she was conscious of being flung across the car as the brakes bit and threw them into a skid, and in the sudden ensuing silence, broken only by a sinister hiss of steam, she became aware of Piers beside her slumped across the steering wheel.

CHAPTER THREE

LOU, for all her emotional timidity, was, curiously enough, undismayed by purely physical shock. Having assured herself that Piers was not dead but merely unconscious she set about determining his injuries. From a nasty-looking cut on his forehead and blood on the splintered driving mirror she deduced that he had been thrown forward and knocked himself out. She began staunching the wound with a handkerchief she found in his breast pocket, relieved that he did not appear to be unduly crushed against the steering wheel, and for the first time that day life took on some sort of reality. Here beside her was no longer the notorious Piers Merrick who gave the orders, but a helpless stranger whose face in oblivion looked oddly defenceless.

As she gently dabbed and mopped, Lou found herself memorizing with tender surprise this unfamiliar aspect of the man she had just married. He looked younger and rather touchingly vulnerable, and with the temporary lifting of the habitual mask which he showed to polite society, he was, she thought, a man it would not be difficult to love, for the face now matched the voice.

"Poor Piers . . ." she murmured compassionately, stroking the lines of his unaware face. "Poor little boy, hitting back at life with your fabulous possessions . . . probably not caring very much about any of them . . ." She did not know why she should think this last, except that she supposed if there was money enough to indulge every whim, values would cease to have importance.

She began to be aware that she must be suffering some measure of delayed shock herself, sitting here pondering on unlikely subjects when she should be going to seek help. She made Piers as comfortable as she could, then got out of the car and went to stand in the road to stop the first passing vehicle. Nothing, she realized, had gone by since the accident, and it seemed to be a lonely stretch of road, not even a highway, but probably one of the many short cuts on which Piers prided himself. A short cut to where, though? She had fallen asleep before asking him again where they were going, and now she did not know in which direction to walk to find the nearest town or village. It had started to spatter with rain again and she stood irresolutely in the cold and darkness, glad of the comfort of Melissa's mink, but reminded anew of her borrowed identity.

While she was still trying to decide which way to take, she saw with relief approaching lights in the distance, and ran into the centre of the road, waving frantically.

The car slowed down and an irritable face peered from the window.

"Can't stop for lifts, I'm in a hurry," an equally irritable masculine voice exclaimed. "Run out of juice, I suppose — just like a woman. I'll notify a garage for you."

"No!" she shouted as he seemed about to drive on. "There's been an accident. My — my husband's hurt."

"Oh, that's different," he said, and backed his car into the side of the road. When he got out he revealed himself as a stocky, middle-aged man with a bustling professional manner that was vaguely familiar, and Lou was not at all surprised when he said: "You're in luck, young lady. I happen to be a doctor."

"What a blessing," she said. "I — I think he's just knocked himself out on the driving mirror, but he's got a nasty cut."

The doctor shot her a quick and slightly puzzled glance. She appeared to him to be very young and, in the circumstances, unnaturally calm.

"H'm . . ." he grunted. "Let's have a look."

She stood watching while he bent over Piers, probing

and examining, fetched his bag from the car when he called for it, catching the smell of antiseptic as he cleaned and dressed the wound.

"No very serious damage, I think, but we'd better get him to the hospital. That cut must be stitched," he said, straightening up. "There may be a bit of concussion. I'll go on ahead and send back an ambulance. You're not hurt yourself?"

"No – no, I don't think so. What is the nearest town? I mean I – I haven't an idea where we are."

"Lexiter's only five miles on."

"Lexiter?"

"Lexiter in Wiltshire. Where were you making for?" he asked impatiently.

"I – I don't know," she answered, and as he saw the sudden blankness in her eyes, his scrutiny became professional again.

"Can't remember, eh? Sure you didn't get a crack on the head?"

"Quite sure – and it isn't that I can't remember. I just never knew."

"H'm ... he grunted again, a suspicion beginning to form at the back of his mind that this was a rather odd set-up. The girl was years younger than her husband, if indeed he was her husband, she kept tugging at her mink coat as if the feel of it was unfamiliar, and his trained eye noticed the newness of her handbag and the luggage piled in the back of the car. At that moment, however, there was a movement from his patient, and he turned back quickly.

"He's coming round," he said. "Hand me that bottle of sal volatile, please."

"Damn cats!" said Piers quite distinctly, and opened his eyes.

"Here, drink this," the doctor said, and smiled a trifle grimly when his patient grimaced with distaste and demanded something stronger.

"Not if there's any chance of concussion," he replied, puzzled by something familiar about the man's face. "There's been a slight accident and you knocked yourself out. How do you feel?"

"Damn silly! I remember now. A cat streaked out of the hedge and I tried to avoid it."

"Never avoid animals when you're driving," the doctor said automatically. "You might have killed your – er – wife."

Piers did not seem to notice the hesitation, but his eyes became alarmed.

"Lou – where is she? Is she all right?" he exclaimed, and Lou, leaning in from the open nearside door, said rather tremulously:

"I'm here, Piers. I'm not hurt."

He put out a hand to touch her, feeling the dampness of rain on the soft fur of the coat.

"Poor Cinderella ..." he murmured. "What a typical ending to the day for you."

The doctor cleared his throat, more certain than ever that something odd was going on, then memory suddenly clicked into place. Piers ... ah, the recent build-up in the gutter press ...

"Aren't you Piers Merrick?" he asked sharply, and Piers grinned.

"Right first time, and I don't doubt you're also aware that I was married today. It only takes a blasted cat to upset one's arrangements, doesn't it?" he said, but the doctor frowned. There had been photographs in plenty of the future Mrs. Merrick, and she bore little resemblance to this uneasy-looking young girl who was now demanding anxiously whether or not the cat had been black.

"How the devil should I know?" Piers retorted irritably. "Everything looks black in the dark. The main thing is to find out how much damage has been done to the car and get going again if we're able."

He began to struggle out of the driving seat and the doctor said with crisp authority:

"You'll come straight to Lexiter Hospital with me, young man. That wound must be stitched, and until you've been X-rayed and okayed, you won't be going anywhere, so let that be clearly understood."

"What in Hades has it got to do with you?" The old arrogance was back in Piers' voice, even though he reached a little unsteadily for support on the car door as he stood up.

"I happen to be a doctor, which, if I may say so, was your good fortune," the other man said. "Now you can walk as far as my car, I think. When I've settled you in safe hands I'll instruct a garage to send out for your car. Mrs. – er – Merrick will of course accompany us."

This time Piers noticed the hesitation and his grin returned.

"Oh, she's my wife all right, but I can understand your confusion, Doctor. All will be revealed to you in the Sunday press, I don't doubt," he said ambiguously, but he allowed himself to be helped into the doctor's car without further protest, and lay back with closed eyes.

"You're remarkably calm, Cinderella," he observed to Lou sitting silently beside him. "No feminine tears? No expressions of thankfulness that you're not so soon a widow?"

"Your wife has an admirable control of her feelings," the doctor snapped from the driving seat. He did not understand the reactions of this uncomfortable pair, presumably on the first stage of their honeymoon, and was anxious to be rid of them.

"Yes, hasn't she?" Piers rejoined, adding in a soft aside that only Lou could hear: "Or perhaps she just doesn't care. That could be it, couldn't it, Cinderella?"

"I wish," said Lou, beginning to feel very tired and

inclined to be tearful after all, "you wouldn't go on calling me that. It isn't true any longer, anyway."

"No, I suppose it isn't. The slipper having fitted, the kitchenmaid becomes a princess."

"I was never a kitchenmaid," Lou protested with the unthinking absurdity of someone too exhausted to be rational any longer.

"Don't be so literal – or so sharp, my poor child," he retorted, but she found her hand suddenly taken in a clasp of reassurance. "Our good Samaritan will think we're quarrelling."

The doctor did, although he could not hear what they said above the noise of the engine. His first suspicions of Lou were, perforce, laid to rest, but he found himself taking a profound dislike to this dark, bitter-tongued fellow who claimed to be her husband. He was not at all sure that the girl hadn't been suffering from shock, after all, declaring halfwittedly that she didn't know where they were going to, and apparently more concerned about a cat's colour than her bridegroom's lucky escape. He wished the hospital staff joy of them; young Merrick, he shrewdly suspected, was too accustomed to getting his own way to be detained against his will without creating a scene.

Piers was, with the one exception that he seldom found it necessary to create scenes. He found no necessity now, when, having submitted gracefully to medical attention, he was pronounced reasonably whole but advised to stay the night for observation and a further check-up in the morning.

"Not on your nelly!" he said. "We've a long drive ahead of us yet, and I don't fancy spending the first night of my honeymoon in a hospital ward – besides, where could you put my wife?"

"Your honeymoon?" frowned the young doctor, prob-

53

ably used to any excuse that would break hospital rules.

"I was married only today. You quite rightly refrain from reading the gossip columns of your daily paper, I must infer, but a bell is beginning to ring for the nurse here, I think," Piers said. The young nurse's eyes had certainly begun to widen in puzzled speculation, but the doctor, who despised the gossip columns and had no intention of being put in his place by a chance casualty, inclined to give himself airs, merely replied coldly:

"You're talking too much as it is, and you're certainly not fit to drive any distance, even if you find your car in running order. How far have you got to go?"

"Cornwall. To a little island called Rune," Piers said with a quick glance at the nurse, who obliged this time with an excited little squeak of recognition.

"You're *the* Mr. Merrick, then!" she exclaimed. "The one all the fuss has been about. It was on the news – the wedding, I mean, and how you married the bride's cousin when everyone thought – "

"Nurse!" The doctor sharply interrupted such unprofessional behaviour in a subordinate, but his eyes traveled over his patient with fresh interest. Despite his contempt for the gossip writers and their usually willing victims, the name of Merrick cropping up from time to time had held a passing interest for him, but for different reasons. A chap who spent mints on yachts, fine cars, financing expeditions, an island on which guests were seldom bidden, rather than on night-clubs and vulgarly lavish parties, at least got a kick out of living. It was said too, though never by the gossip writers, that Piers Merrick did a great amount of charitable good with his money and never claimed notoriety for it.

"Well, Mr. Merrick," he said more pleasantly, "I can't force you to remain here, but I must insist that you stay in Lexiter at least for the night. There may be some delayed concussion, though I personally don't think that will arise, but one can't be too careful, and I would like you to come back here in the morning for a final check-up."

"And where would you suggest I start my honeymoon?" Piers asked with his little twisted smile.

"Lexiter is a big town. There are several good hotels," the doctor replied stiffly, and Piers gave him one of his unexpected and totally disarming grins.

"Of course there are — and thank you for all your trouble. I'll be back in the morning," he said, and young Doctor Evans found himself shaking hands with an unaccustomed warmth, aware that the young nurse had already disappeared in a hurry, presumably to get a look at the bride.

Lou sat stiffly on one of the straight-backed chairs that lined the walls of the waiting-room. People had offered her cups of tea and proffered magazines, but she just sat there staring at the blank wall ahead with eyes that no longer seemed to focus very well.

It was, she thought, trying to co-ordinate the day's happenings into some sort of order, all part of the dream. Nothing had been real since yesterday, nothing, perhaps, would ever be real again. She had been calm when the accident happened because that also had seemed part of the dream. When the little nurse looked in, accompanied by others to whom she had imparted the news, she was beginning to wonder if, indeed, she had been living in a state of trauma and quite soon she would waken to the dull but familiar life she had always known.

"Mrs. Merrick?" the first nurse said. "Your husband is just coming. We do think it's a shame that your honeymoon should be spoilt like this, but he's all right. You were going to the island, weren't you?"

This time, Lou at least had the wit not to answer that she didn't know, and on the face of it, it would seem sensible that Piers had abandoned his plans for a continental honeymoon.

"Yes," she said, trying to smile, "we were going to the island."

"It's ever so exciting," one of the nurses giggled. "Switching brides and all, I mean – it was on the news this evening – did you know?"

"No, I didn't," said Lou, who had been unaware of the television unit outside the church, and jumped more than the nurses when a biting voice observed from the doorway:

"What are you girls doing here? Kindly return to your duties at once, and report to me in the morning."

"Yes, Sister," they replied with one accord, and disappeared, leaving Lou with a middle-aged woman who, despite her starch and air of authority, suddenly twinkled at Lou.

"One can't blame them being curious, Mrs. Merrick," she said. "You and your husband have certainly made the headlines today."

"Have we?" asked Lou vaguely, and the other woman gave her a quick, clinical glance.

"Well, of course, you must know that," she said. "I think, in all the attention your husband has commanded, we've forgotten you might be suffering from shock. How do you feel, my dear?"

"Quite all right, thank you. I only want to – want to – "

"Want to what?"

"Just know where I shall end the day."

Sister's eyes rested with sympathetic but false understanding on the bride's pale, childish face. What bad luck, she thought, to be stranded in a town like Lexiter for that all-important start to a marriage, when, with a bridegroom like Piers Merrick, the honeymoon would have been planned with the maximum degree of luxury.

"Well, I'm afraid our best hotel is all that can be offered in the circumstances," she said, "but the Queen's is comfortable and too expensive for local pockets, so you should be all right."

"It doesn't really matter any more, does it?" said Lou in a thin little thread of a voice, and Sister was relieved to see the girl's husband, preceded by the doctor, entering the room.

"Doctor – " she whispered quickly, "I think Mrs. Merrick should have attention, and perhaps a sedative. She seems – " But Lou rose rather stiffly to her feet and held out her hands to Piers.

"They say you're all right. Are you, Piers? The garage have overhauled the car and they say it's fit to drive. Are we going on?"

He made a quick step towards her, taking her out-stretched hands in his, and the two people watching received each in their different ways an uneasy feeling that all was not right, but that at the same time there was something rather touching in the way the weary-looking man had taken the hands of his young and unresponsive bride. The young doctor saw that the bride seemed in a state of suspension, and resolved to find out from the nurses what stories the avid press were putting about.

"You're sure you feel all right, Mrs. Merrick?" he said. "You wouldn't care to have the rule run over you, just in case?"

"No," she said faintly, but quite firmly. "I'm only tired. It's – it's been a long day."

"Yes, a long day, poor Cinderella," Piers said gently, "but it will soon be over. Could I make arrangements with an hotel from here, Doctor Evans?"

"It's already been done," the doctor returned a little gruffly. "The Queen's have reserved their best room for you – the hotels are fairly empty at this time of year. Now, Mr. Merrick, you'll return tomorrow for that check-up, please?"

"Yes, I'll be back," Piers answered, and put an arm round Lou's shoulders, guiding her to the door.

Lexiter was, as the doctor had said, a big town, and

the hotel at which their taxi deposited them an imposing if hideous example of the Edwardian era. The interior was equally ugly with its marble floors and pillars, the plush and gilt which looked outdated and rather gloomy, palms in gigantic pots and tiers of stiffly planted flower-boxes.

"We have given you the Bridal Suite, naturally, Mr Merrick. Such an unfortunate setback to your plans but, if I may say so, a fortunate turn of events for the Queen's – ha, ha . . ." the manager said, conducting them personally to their rooms.

"Why? Do you propose putting up a plaque stating that Mr. Merrick slept here?" asked Piers innocently, and the manager laughed again somewhat nervously. He and his whole staff had been delighted at an unexpected share in the publicity following the wedding of the year, but the legendary Piers Merrick hardly looked his best with lint and plaster over one temple, and the bride, for all her mink and expensive accessories, had the air of a dressed-up child obediently following instructions.

"Well," said Piers, surveying their quarters with a quiz-zical expression, "I've never occupied a bridal suite before, have you?"

"Of course not," Lou replied, thinking the question foolish in the circumstances, and he stood watching with a faint smile, while she tentatively explored the suite's potentialities. Sitting-room, bedroom, dressing-room, dis-played the same faded grandeur as the rest of the hotel, but the manager must have sent out hurriedly for flowers, for they filled the suite in hastily arranged abundance, and their heavy scent reminded Lou of the funereal impression she had received yesterday from Cousin Blanche's decked-out drawing-room.

"It feels like a conservatory," she said, and he opened a window.

"Central heating going full blast, but it's preferable to

freezing in the arctic chambers of most provincial morgues,'' he said, and watched her eyes slide away from the vast double bed to their joint possessions already unpacked and distributed in appropriate places.

"Can you remember a time when you hadn't all this, Piers?" she asked, observing with surprise that whereas all her expensive toilet accessories were new and clearly meant to impress, his brushes and other masculine requirements were well-worn and unpretentious.

"Oh, yes. We were comfortable, I suppose, but not well off until my father inherited from that forgotten black sheep of the family who took himself off to the wilds of Australia or somewhere and made a fortune no one believed in till he died. I must have been about twelve or so. The principal difference it made to me then was the fact that my father altered his original plans for my education and sent me to a famous public school he could never have afforded otherwise – a fact, I may say, not at all appreciated by me at the time.'' He was talking easily and with patience, for he thought, watching her changing expression as her gaze wandered round the room, that she was just beginning to realize that she was irrevocably committed, that their intimate possessions cheek by jowl together bore mute testimony that the pretence was over, that reality must be faced, and that for her reality might be frightening.

She was still wearing her coat and he slipped it gently off her shoulders, letting it fall in a rich, supple heap on the floor as he turned her round to face him.

"Lou – " he said, " – are you scared?"

He could have shaken her as her eyes met his rather blankly. Couldn't she understand that he was trying to make things easy for her? Then she confounded him with one of those calm flashes of maturity he had not yet come to expect from her.

"Yes," she replied quite simply. "I'm scared. Not for the

– the conventional reasons, but because you're a stranger, and someone quite out of my world. I may not measure up."

He should, he know, have felt compassion, even been touched by a humility he had not met with in other women, but his head was beginning to throb unmercifully and he was merely irritated.

"Don't be humble, Cinderella," he said a little harshly. "I wouldn't care for a sacrificial doormat, however pleasing to one's ego for a time."

Her eyes flew open in sudden shock, or perhaps it was simply hurt surprise, but she said nothing and he observed more gently:

"I suppose we should be thinking about dinner. No doubt our rather fulsome manager would be delighted to serve us something in our rooms, but I think we'll grace the public dining-room just the same."

"Should I change?" she asked like a child unsure of correct procedure.

"If you like," he replied indifferently, and reflected that she was again like a child, stripping off her suit without embarrassment, wandering about in her slip apparently unconscious of the fact that he stood and watched her. She was most delicately made, he thought, observing the small bones which, like those of a young cat, lent grace to movement, even though not fully matured, and he began to regret his decision to dine in public.

When she was ready she slowly turned herself about for his approval, and looked disappointed when he said briefly: "Not your colour." No, she thought, it was Melissa's colour, it was part of Melissa's trousseau; the very brushes she had used, the scent from the jewelled-topped flask, were all part of the extravagant luxuries meant for another bride. If, thought Lou unhappily, I had just *something* of my own that wasn't bought for someone else....

"I believe you're vain, Cinderella," Piers teased, trying to guess from her changing expressions what she was thinking. "Are you hurt because I don't care for your dress?"

"Why should I be? It was made for Melissa," she replied, and as the amusement left his face, wished she had not pointed this out

"I – Cousin Blanche didn't think my own clothes would be suitable, you see," she said, trying to explain what must seem to him a liberty, but he merely looked bored

"My dear child, you don't have to apologise. As I gather I'm being soaked for the lot, I couldn't care less. Come on, let's go down. I shall be intrigued to find out what the chef has thought up as a honeymoon offering."

"Will there be something special, then?"

"I don't mind betting there will. This rather dreary hotel will flourish for weeks on tall stories circulating about the Merricks' bridal night. Come on."

She went with him to wait for the lift to take them down, feeling at last that she wanted to weep, to plead, not for consideration in the expected culmination of the day, but for comfort. She would have liked him to understand that although she wore Melissa's clothes, and used her expensive appointments, she was still herself, Cinderella perhaps, but not liking or wanting her borrowed finery. She wished that Piers' unfortunate accident gave her the right to comfort and cosset in her turn, but he did not seem receptive to sentiment, neither was he prone to weakness. For him the interruption of his plans amused rather than upset him, for a honeymoon designed along quite different lines could nor longer have any importance for him.

They sat in the lofty, almost deserted dining-room, making polite conversation. The chef, as Piers had surmised, had surpassed himself in the dishes that were offered. Lou, who was now too tired to be appreciative or, indeed, to enjoy the inspired creations of the cuisine, picked at her food and earned frowning diapproval from Piers.

"They really have rather excelled themselves," he said. "Make a pretence of eating, Lou, or the chef will be, not unnaturally, insulted."

She made a pretence, hoping that the bits she hid under her knife and fork would not be noticed. She was, she thought, looking at her husband's frowning face, going to find it difficult to acquire his epicurean habits when her own tastes in the matter of food had been so sadly neglected.

He had ordered champagne because, he said, it was expected of him. For his own pleasure, he would have proffered a vintage claret.

"Then why didn't you?" she asked, and he smiled that little twisted smile that, this time, held no tenderness.

"Champagne is what you expected too, isn't it? You have got to be educated in the matter of wines."

"Of course," she said, clinging on to the tattered remnants of her past self, "you must remember that I've had little opportunity of being educated to your standards. In my parents' lifetime, a cheap sherry was all we could afford."

His look of amusement vanished and, for a moment, she thought his eyes were humble.

"You put me in my place very neatly, don't you, Cinderella?" he said gently. "I wasn't, you know, trying to point out your mistakes."

"Mistakes? Am I shaming you, then, already, Piers?"

"Don't be so idiotic! I hoped I might put you at ease, that's all. What's wrong with cheap sherry if you can't afford anything else?"

"Nothing, I suppose," she replied nervously. "Only – "

"Only what?"

"Only you don't put me at ease when you pounce and bite."

"Pounce and bite — is that what I did?" He sounded surprised and his eyes softened into tenderness.

She saw the tenderness, but it was too late now to set any store by it. She had, she told herself with wry humour, married above her station, as the gossip columns would surely imply; Cinderella would have to look to herself for wisdom in dealing with her Prince Charming, for there was no one else to advise.

"What were you thinking?" he asked, but she smiled a little uncertainly and shook her head. Such thoughts were hardly to be expressed with any clarity, neither did she feel he would understand. She did not understand a great deal herself, now she came to think of it, only a firm resolve that he should not find her wanting when it came to the test, that whatever his reasons for so casually putting her in Melissa's place, he had still been the first man to stir her.

He did not repeat his question when she did not answer, but caught the head waiter's attention with a small imperious nod. The chef was summoned and graciously congratulated, the wine waiter rewarded and dismissed with pleasant thanks, even the scullery hands were fetched from the kitchen because, said Piers, they really did all the work. It was the first time Lou had witnessed the famous Merrick charm turned on like a tap, and she watched and listened with a twinge of embarrassment. They might have been royalty, she thought, and indeed royalty could not have been more obsequiously received.

"Do you always do this?" she asked as they left the dining-room, and saw one eyebrow lifted in wry amusement.

"You think it was a bit overdone?" he said. "Perhaps it was — still, we've inadvertently made their day, and they've all been falling over backwards to please."

"People always fall over backwards for you, Piers, I imagine," she said, and he made a small grimace.

"Well, money buys most things, I've always found. You'll learn that too when you've got used to being the wife of a rich man," he retorted with a certain astringence, but if he thought he had dashed an ill-timed hint of criticism, he had misjudged Lou's innocent tenacity.

"I don't think I'll learn easily. I wouldn't want bought affection," she said, and looked surprised when he stopped dead in their leisurely passage towards the lift.

"And what do you mean by that?" he demanded with an ominous change of tone. "Are you suggesting, for instance, that I've bought your affection, if, that is, I can flatter myself that you feel any affection towards me?"

She felt herself colouring under his cynical gaze, aware that she had surprisingly managed to hurt him, that for all his boasting to the contrary, he could still expect something that was not to be bought.

"I wasn't thinking of us. I – I was speaking generally," she stammered, aware that she had such little knowledge of men that she was almost bound to say the wrong thing.

"Then you should be thinking of us. You should be thinking very seriously of our future and all it may entail," he said, and she could see out of the corner of her eye that a page-boy and two waitresses were affording them curious if discreet attention.

"Yes ... yes, I should," she agreed hurriedly. "Piers, people are listening. Oughtn't we – oughtn't we to go up?"

"Perhaps you'd rather sit in the lounge and postpone the evil hour," he said, and she wondered for a fleeting moment if, after all, he was as nervous as she, then inwardly laughed at herself for such an absurd notion. The wedding night of a man as experienced in casual love affairs as Piers Merrick was reputed to be would scarcely hold any doubts or fears.

"No," she said, "let's go up. You – you ought to have an early night, surely, after that crack on the head?"

She saw the little unamused smile he gave her, but he moved on towards the lift without making any immediate reply. Only when the door of their suite had closed behind them did he return to a subject she had hoped forgotten because it could well have been misunderstood.

"Poor Cinderella," he said, taking her by the shoulders. "Were you hoping to pack your bridegroom off to an early bed and so avoid the consequences? My crack on the head hasn't incapacitated me, you know."

She stood looking uncertainly up into his face.

"Piers . . ." she began hesitantly, "I just don't know how to answer you. . . . I've married you, and anything you choose to ask of me I'll gladly give you. That – that affection you spoke of downstairs – it's true I – I wouldn't have married you just to get Cousin Blanche out of a jam, or – or for mercenary reasons. Happiness can't be bought."

"A cliché, old as the hills."

"But true."

"Perhaps." He took her face between hands which were gentle and suddenly unsure. "You're very sweet," he said, "very sweet, and deserving of a better husband than you've got, I'm afraid. We were both a little mad, perhaps."

"Are you regretting things?"

"I never regret things. If they don't work out, I just forget them, or throw them away."

"Oh . . . is that a warning?"

"Not, I think, in the sense you mean," he told her with gentle amusement, but Lou was not so sure. The very rich could afford to indulge their whims and follies. Hadn't he said that money could buy most things? A handsome settlement, a few costly presents, and even an ill-chosen wife could be discarded.

"You're very tired, aren't you, Lou?" he said, understanding too late that his approach had been quite wrong. He should have ordered dinner up here, made love to her, wakened her out of the dream they had all forced upon

65

her. He felt suddenly inexplicably humbled by her honesty, her uninformed efforts to please him. Pride and anger had driven him to this outrageous gesture, but he thought as he observed the shadows under her eyes, and felt the weariness in her passive, unresisting young body, that he had not been altogether wrong when he had told her she might be what he needed.

She would not, however, admit she was tired, fearing he would take it as an excuse, but when he pulled her down on to a sofa and drew her head against his shoulder, comforting but quite impersonal, she said impulsively:

"I know so little about you, Piers – tell me things."

"What do you want to know?"

"Tell me about the island," she said, sensing that the island was in some curious fashion part of himself.

"Rune?"

"That's where we're going, isn't it? One of the nurses told me."

"One of the nurses?" There was both puzzlement and displeasure in his voice and she could already feel the familiar withdrawal in him.

"She took it for granted, naturally, that I knew where my honeymoon was to be spent," she replied demurely, but she could no longer, it appeared, provoke him to amused retaliation, and when he next spoke it was with rather formal politeness.

"I'm sorry if you find my change of plans dull," he said, "but I didn't imagine you and Melissa would share the same tastes when it came to – er – honeymoons."

It was the first time he had deliberately mentioned Melissa, and it seemed to Lou to bring her into the room, pointing, a jeering ghost, at the dim little cousin who wore her clothes and her wedding ring and imagined she could take her place. Piers, of course, must be regretting his hasty act of bravado: no wonder he had decided that it was better to return at once to the island, rather than waste time and money on the lavish and protracted honeymoon he had planned for somebody else. And that, too, was an act of defiance, for he and Melissa had quarrelled about the island.

She got to her feet and started to unzip her dress. Someone, after all, had to make the first move to bring this difficult day to its logical climax, and she did not know how to make it clear to Piers that although she could not aspire to Melissa's skill in handling such matters, she was a willing and ready pupil.

"What a ridiculous word honeymoon is," she said brightly, struggling rather unsuccessfully with the zip which seemed out of reach after a certain distance.

"Yes, it is rather," he agreed, and the amusement was back in his voice as he very expertly completed the operation for her.

I wonder how many women ... she began thinking to herself, and blushed as she read in his eyes that he was quite aware of her thoughts. He wandered into the bedroom, flicked the elaborate nightgown laid out on the bed with an inquisitive finger, then gathered up his own pyjamas and disappeared into the dressing-room.

Lou undressed with speed, spending little time with Melissa's creams and lotions because she had never acquired the habit of expensive cosmetics. Every so often her wedding ring fell off as it had done throughout the evening; it would be safer, she thought, to leave it on the dressing-table than lose it in the bed. She pulled on Melissa's nightdress, the last reminder of the day of her lost identity, and got into bed.

She seemed to wait a long time for Piers. He was, she supposed uneasily, used to women who took hours making themselves alluring for him, whereas she had not thought to follow other than her nightly routine of soap and water and a good hair brushing. But even as she was preparing to make a hurried dart for her lipstick and a dab of scent, he came into the room and stood there looking down at her.

"I was – I was just going to put on some scent," she said rather idiotically, and his smile had the old touch of tenderness as he observed her anxious face. She was looking like a good little girl, he thought, clean and brushed for the night, waiting to be kissed and tucked up.

"Were you, indeed?" he said. "Well, there's always tomorrow."

"T – tomorrow?"

"To try out the scent. What are you staring at? Does the not very glamorous sticking plaster spoil your romantic illusions?"

"No. It makes you look rather like a pirate, as a matter of fact – that very gorgeous dressing gown and the crimson scarf tucked in."

"A shade ostentatious, you think?"

"Oh, no, not at all. A little flamboyance suits your raffish air."

"Have I a raffish air?"

"You know quite well you have. I think you rather trade on it."

"This," he remarked, sitting down on the bed, "is rather a curious turn for the conversation to take, don't you think? One doesn't expect one's newly wedded wife to take one to task so soon."

Didn't he understand, she thought, that she was talking nonsense to cover her nervousness?

"I'm sorry," she said, twisting the sheet unhappily in her thin, ringless fingers, and in spite of himself his irritation returned, together with a renewed throbbing in his head.

"Don't be so naïve, I was only joking," he said sharply. "Where's your wedding ring?"

"It kept dropping off, so I left it on the dressing-table," she said. "It was Melissa's, wasn't it?"

"Yes, it was Melissa's. I must get you another." He spoke with indifference, and she knew she had been wrong to remind him of Melissa. For all Cousin Blanche's assertion that the engagement had been one of mutual convenience rather than something deeper, it could not be pleasant, she thought, to picture the bride of your choice enjoying your privileges with another man. She could not tell him this but, mistakenly, she tried to make him understand her own difficulties.

"You see," she said, "everything I have with me is Melissa's. I – I feel like a – an understudy. I'm not what you wanted and I'm not me any more . . . can't you understand, Piers?"

"I understand perfectly," he replied, getting to his feet. "It wasn't a fair exchange, was it – the dross for the gold, the lioness for the lamb?"

"I don't understand you," she faltered. "I wanted . . . I was willing . . . I *am* willing . . ."

"Of course you are, my poor innocent, but if you will excuse my lack of ardour on such an occasion, I'll go to my bed," he said, adding as her eyes slid to the empty place beside her, "Next door. That crack on the head was convenient for you, after all, wasn't it, my sweet? Goodnight. God bless."

"Take care of yourself," Lou answered as he bent and kissed her, because it was the familiar tag which sped any departing guest, then as their dividing door closed behind him, she turned her face into the pillow and wept for her own inadequacy.

CHAPTER FOUR

THEY arrived at their destination on the following evening. Piers had kept his appointment with the hospital in the morning, but since he had been pronounced fit to drive, he had seen no reason to linger for another day in Lexiter.

Lou, who had slept badly, found him a morose travelling companion. Only when they reached the ragged beginnings of the Cornish coast did he seem to become aware of her, pointing out this and that landmark in the gathering dusk, manoeuvring the car with skill but alarming speed through high-banked lanes which, to her unaccustomed eyes, looked too narrow to accommodate one vehicle, let alone another coming from the opposite direction.

"What happens if we meet something?" she asked.

"Someone has to back. Haven't you noticed the bays cut in the banks?"

"No, I hadn't. Oh, yes, I see – there's one. How twisty the road is. When will we see the sea?"

"In a little while. Haven't you been to Cornwall before?"

He seemed pleased when she told him she hadn't, and she thought there was altogether a new warmth in his voice as he answered her questions, as if he were approaching a secret treasure of his own, and she remembered her old impression that the island was, for him, both an escape and a refuge.

"Tell me about Rune," she said, but his answer lacked encouragement, or perhaps he was simply reluctant to share his own delight in the island.

"You probably won't care for Rune," he replied with a certain austerity. "It's a very small island offering no amusements one can't make for oneself."

"Such as?"

"Fishing, sailing, bird-watching for anyone interested. At this time of the year, the weather becomes rough, and Rune can be cut off from the mainland by storms. The winter can be long and harsh."

"Are we going to spend the winter there?" She asked the question in all good faith, but he shot her a swift look as if he detected a demure amusement in her.

"How would you react if I answered yes?" he replied. "You don't, perhaps, take my island kingdom very seriously."

"I haven't," she returned politely, "had time to think about it. I didn't, after all, know where we were going when we started out."

"Neither you did. Are you feeling I've cheated you out of the conventional honeymoon – Paris, bright lights, luxury hotels?" There was a cynical bite to his voice as if he rather enjoyed the implication that his change of bride had automatically brought about a change in his plans. Melissa would never have consented to spend one night of her honeymoon on an island cut off from civilization, thought Lou, but Melissa, of course, had been consulted in the proper manner.

"Well, are you?" Piers asked impatiently as, occupied with her own thoughts, she made no reply.

"You can't feel cheated out of something you never expected," she said then, and he gave a slight smile.

"True," he replied rather dryly, and she reflected that he might well be thinking that this also could apply to himself.

The road which had been winding uphill for some time now suddenly converged into open country, banks gave way to low stone walls, and quite suddenly Lou seemed to be on the edge of the world.

"There's the sea for you," Piers said, stopping the car.

They were at the top of a great chain of cliffs, stretching

jaggedly into the distance, with the road like a torn thread running ahead through the falling darkness. The sound of the breakers far below and the wind whining across miles of desolate country sent a momentary shiver of apprehension through Lou. Such complete isolation with a stranger whose moods, she felt, could well match this savage territory brought the first doubts to her mind.

"Cold?" he asked, aware that very much earlier he had put down the hood of the car without reference to her comfort.

"No."

"Scared, then?"

She answered, as before, quite simply: "Yes, I am a little scared. This country is as strange to me as you are. I – I may not measure up."

"So you've said before. And you think Melissa would?"

She could not picture her pleasure-seeking cousin putting up for very long with nature in the raw, but she only replied gently:

"Melissa can measure up to most things, I should think. You didn't anyway, I imagine, suggest bringing her here for a honeymoon."

He gave her another of those quick little glances as if those apparently innocent observations puzzled him.

"That," he said, "would have been asking a little much of both of us."

"What an odd thing to say."

"Is it? I had no illusions about the fair Melissa. She had it all nicely worked out that she would, in due course, persuade me to sell Rune, so the longer I kept her away from the island the longer the inevitable clash would be postponed. Rune would have bored her to tears."

He sounded so bitter when Melissa's name was mentioned that Lou thought Cousin Blanche must be mistaken when she had declared this to be no love match on Piers' side. It was not pleasant, the youngest bridesmaid thought uneasily, to be married out of pique and share the bridegroom with the ghost of his rightful bride. Lou pulled the borrowed mink more closely about her, shivering again, and in one of those strange moments of perception, he cupped her chin in his hand and turned her face up to his.

"You feel I've taken an unfair advantage, don't you?" he said. "You think because I'm bringing you straight to Rune I don't consider you worth spending money or trouble on. You couldn't be more wrong. When you know me better you'll understand I'm paying you a compliment."

She experienced a rush of warmth towards him, for there was the promise of comfort in his suddenly intent regard, tenderness in the light touch of his fingers.

"Because you're willing to share your island with me?" she asked shyly. He was, everyone said, absurdly jealous of his rights over his small kingdom.

"Perhaps," he replied with an enigmatic little smile, "but that will be up to you, my dear."

So it was to be a testing time for her, she thought, feeling unexpectedly angry, and when she spoke he heard with surprise the change in her voice.

"It will be up to you too, Piers. You married me," she said, and he turned the ignition key with a click of finality as if anxious to end a conversation that was becoming too personal.

"So I did. You must remind me of that from time to time," he said, and drove on.

It was quite dark when they reached the tiny hamlet of St. Bede from where Piers said a launch would take them to the island. A boatman was waiting at the jetty, but there was no one else about. Lou stood on the little stone pier straining her eyes to see if she could make out the shape of the island in the darkness while the luggage was unloaded from the car. The broad, silent Cornishman had greeted Piers monosyllabically, glanced incuriously at his bride, then steadied the launch as Piers picked Lou up and swung her over the side. She sat where she was told, feeling the spray on her face and the wind in her hair, wondering how far they had to go. Piers took the helm himself while the boatman got a pipe going, then settled from habit into the role of passenger. Nobody spoke at all.

Their passage took little time, for the island was not much more than a mile out from the mainland, and presently Lou could see lights and a dark mass lying like some strange monster in the water, and a sense of excitement gripped her. Was it not a perfectly natural sequence in the fairy tale to be brought by boat to an island and the unknown fastness of the Prince's castle?

She disembarked clumsily, not waiting for a steadying hand, in her eagerness to set foot on Rune, and fell awkwardly on the slippery cobbles.

"For heaven's sake don't make a habit of that until you're more practised with boats or you'll find yourself in the drink," Piers rebuked her sharply, then turned to greet and then accompany a couple of men with the luggage up to the house, either forgetting or ignoring her.

Lou followed them, feeling a little crestfallen and slipping every so often on the rough stones which formed steps up to a small terrace. For a moment she experience a pang of disappointment, for the house, built of the local stone and slate, was stark and unimposing and not very big. She had, she supposed, so convinced of the story-book unreality of the past three days, expected a castle with turrets and battlements and even a drawbridge. Piers, turning, saw the look on her face as she stood staring in the lamplight which flooded out of the open door, and laughed aloud.

"My poor Cinderella, were you expecting a palace?" he said. "You'll find my home very simple and unpretentious, I'm afraid. Come on in and get the feel of the house."

He was over the threshold, holding the door for her, and as he saw her hesitate his smile became a little mocking.

"Are you superstitious, Lou? Well, I can oblige you over one of the many conventions I seem to have cheated you out of," he said, and picking her up, carried her over the threshold.

She was pliant and incredibly light in his arms, but as he put her down he felt her sudden withdrawal.

"That wasn't necessary," she said, trying to match his own barely concealed impatience with traditional customs.

"But you expected it, didn't you? You've expected a good many things that I've failed to appreciate, I'm afraid."

"I've expected nothing," she said sturdily, blinking back the tears which she had fought back too long and too valiantly. Such a little thing to make one want to weep, such an empty gesture of convention to please a bride who knew too well that she meant little or nothing to a man who was simply paying off old scores.

"Then you must mend your ways, Cinderella," he said softly. "If you expect nothing you get nothing – only pumpkins and white mice. Come along and meet Tibby, for you'll need her approval far more than you'll need mine."

Lou, her courage nearly drained, did not feel that she made much of a hit with Tibby. She came from the back regions, presumably the kitchen, to meet them, a thin, rather gaunt old woman, very upright and very observant. She had, it transpired, been Piers' nurse, but had kept house for him on the island ever since he bought it. It seemed odd to Lou, trying to make the right responses, to think of Piers with a nanny, and she, who had never known one of her own, was disappointed in Tibby as she had been disappointed in the house. Nannies, she had vaguely supposed, were plump and comfortable, and when one retired, indulgent recipients of confidences, ready to spoil because it no longer mattered, but Tibby invited none of these imageries. She welcomed Piers with pleasure but reserve, and turned an appraising eye on his bride. Lou immediately felt she was found wanting. If Tibby had ever met Melissa, indeed, even if she had not, she was bound to make comparisons.

"I'd have thought you'd more sense, Mr. Piers," was her first uncompromising comment. "Cradle-snatching's the first sign of old age. What possessed you?"

"I don't know, Tibby, unless I had a sudden moment of intuition," Piers answered lazily.

"Intuition, my foot! Temper more like – I've read the papers."

"You should never believe all you read in the press, Tibby dear, and you must be nice to my little bride. She has much to learn about our life here."

"She'll learn nothing you're not willing to teach yourself, but that, most like, will amuse you for a time."

"You will have gathered that Tibby has a poor opinion of me as a prospective husband," he said, cocking an eyebrow at Lou, and she had the unhappy impression that they were both merely using her as the excuse for a familiar sparring match, and she wondered how Melissa would have dealt with this old woman who clearly had little respect or patience for tender feelings. But Melissa, of course, would not have cared. She would have made a few gracious overtures because it was a good thing to be charming to servants, then written Tibby off as a tiresome old bore and tried to persuade Piers to pension her off.

Too tired to pay attention to their voices any longer, Lou let her eyes wander over her new home, or as much of it as she could see from where they stood. *Get the feel of the house*, Piers had said, and she began to realize that the disappointing façade had been misleading. The house had a depth one would not suspect from the front, or someone had built on and created a surprising illusion of space. Stone passages led off the wide hall, high and vaulted, with steps going up and steps going down to other rooms; a great stove, ugly but efficient, radiated a comforting warmth, and oil lamps cast distorted shadows on the white-washed walls.

"Rather bare and monastic, are you thinking?" Piers said suddenly, making her jump, and she became aware that they were both watching her, Piers with a hint of amusement, Tibby with pursed lips and an expression that could be termed pawky. It could matter to neither of them, she reflected, what she thought of the house, so she said nothing.

"You'll be wanting your room, maybe?" the old woman said with a belated sense of her duties, and without waiting for an answer led the way upstairs.

The room Lou found herself in was high and narrow with rush matting covering the floor and a bed that looked comfortable but unwelcoming with its utilitarian air of severity, and plain, dark spread. A door leading to another room stood ajar, and through it Lou glimpsed firelight flickering on Persian rugs and the gleaming patina of polished wood, a room to which this bare, impersonal chamber was clearly an annexe.

"Would you like me to unpack for you?" Tibby said, and Lou caught hostility beneath an offer which was, she was sure, not intended to be taken seriously.

"No, thank you," she replied politely, accepting with a sinking heart the fact that the old woman seemed to have taken a dislike to her, then she became aware that Piers had followed them up and was standing in the doorway with raised eyebrows.

"Why haven't you had the bed moved?" he asked.

"Time enough in the morning," Tibby replied. "You'll be needing a good night's sleep with that bad head and all."

"Stubborn old bitch, aren't you?" Piers observed with the unoffensive ease of long standing. "Well, take Mrs. Merrick's cases into the other room, and bring mine in here. Did you give the orders where she was to sleep?"

"I put you in your accustomed room, naturally, but if madam wishes to change – "

But it appeared to Lou that Piers, too, had caught the scarcely veiled mockery behind that subservient "madam", for his mood changed with alarming swiftness from tolerance to anger.

"We're not back in the nursery now, Tibby," he said with all his old arrogance. "You will have to control your jealousy if you want to remain with us."

"Jealous? Me?"

"Yes, you, and I won't tolerate it. You've been the only woman here for too long, and you know it. You might have a more generous welcome for my wife than this."

"The wife you should have married would never have lived here," the old woman muttered bitterly. "Rune was quite safe from her sort. She'd know her right place in your life. Threw you over, Piers, didn't she, like her mother served your father, and you, for sheer spite, took the little cousin who most likely doesn't know she's born."

"That's enough!" Piers snapped, and at the same time Lou, distracted almost to tears, cried:

"Oh, please stop, both of you. I don't care where I sleep, if that's what's started all this. Miss Tibby, I'm sorry if you resent me, but please, please go away now."

The old woman's shadow was gaunt and forbidding on the wall as she moved towards the door and her cold eyes flicked over Lou without sign of apology.

"Very well," was all she said, and she silently left the room.

"Don't try to soften Tibby by apologising for yourself. She'll only despise you," Piers said, and at last Lou's crumbling defences broke.

She stood with the tears pouring down her face and great tearing sobs choking the words she hurled at him. Wasn't it enough, she cried, that she had married him to save his face and her cousin's threatened disgrace? Hadn't she deputised long enough for another woman, wearing her clothes, borrowing her identity, asking for little in exchange but kindness and consideration?

"It's all your fault!" she finished. "The almighty Merrick arrogance that thinks money can buy anything . . . the disregard for any feelings but your own. Melissa's well out of it . . . sheer spite, that old woman said . . . well, it isn't very nice to be married for spite . . ."

He had listened without interruption, his eyes changing from surprise to gravity as they watched her face. Once or twice his mouth tightened as if with pain, and once or twice he smiled with faint indulgence.

"Well, now – " he said when she had finished, " – how you do surprise me, Cinderella. I wouldn't have thought you had such venom in you."

"Venom?"

"Well, perhaps that's a little strong – such bottled-up resentment, shall we say? Do you really think I married you to spite Melissa?"

"I – I didn't say that."

"But who else could I spite, if that was my reason?"

She was silent, and he took her hands, feeling how cold they were, and led her into the other room. When he had gently thrust her into a chair by the fire he fetched brandy from an old wine-cooler which also appeared to hold the usual bathroom assortment of bottles and first-aid appliances, and while she sipped her drink, changed over the suitcases from one room to the other, and removed the clean pyjamas already laid out on the turned-down bed which Lou saw was a twin to the one next door.

"Yes, the other one belongs in here," he said, observing her look. "I only had it moved out because if you sleep alone a second empty bed is depressing, don't you think? Shall I unpack for you?"

It was such an uncharacteristic domestic suggestion that

she smiled through her tears, but shook her head. He was, she knew, giving her time to recover composure by making casual, mundane observations as he moved between the two rooms, and she was touched by a forbearance she had not learnt to expect from him.

"Tomorrow we'll get properly organised," he said, unlocking the cases for her. "Tibby must have misunderstood my instructions." It was a kindly prevarication, she thought, but one neither of them believed. Tibby had made it her business to ensure that Lou's second night of marriage should be as abortive as the first.

"Better?" Piers asked, taking the empty glass from her, and when she nodded, giving him rather a watery smile, came and sat on the arm of her chair.

"Lou – " he began a little tentatively, " – I feel I should disabuse you of certain misconceptions."

"Yes?" The moment suddenly held promise, and she rubbed her cheek against his sleeve like a little ingratiating cat.

"I don't want you to think that spite entered into my sudden change of plans. The spite was Tibby's, and that, I'm afraid, is a problem you'll have to sort out between you. Tibby would have taken more kindly to Melissa because she felt it was a settling of old scores. She was very attached to my father, and I suppose she had some muddled notion that the next generation could cancel out."

"And hadn't you that notion, Piers?" she asked, trying to reconcile all the puzzling facets of this affair into something she could understand.

"Yes, I suppose I had. Melissa is very like Blanche at the same age, you know, and – a small boy's first impressions of the perfect woman can be lasting."

"Sublimation, or something?"

"I expect so. The trick-cyclists would have a name for it."

"They would say it was unconscious transference of a

mother complex," Lou said, and giggled sleepily at the unlikely thought of Melissa providing maternal solace to any man she married.

"Very likely," he said somewhat sharply, "but I was not, I assure you, thinking in those terms when I got engaged to your cousin. I wanted to settle down, found a family, to leave something worthwhile behind me. The old ties, being such as they were, and Blanche ready and eager to bargain, my course seemed simple."

"It's not simple to me," Lou said. "Why are you explaining all this? You loved Melissa, surely?"

He moved a little impatiently.

"Because, I suppose, my motives are still the same. I want to settle down, and you, my little Cinderella, are nobly filling the gap. Melissa is damned attractive, and I admit to being more than narked at being let down at the last minute, but I thought I had made it clear that you were not chosen at random — added to which, you didn't have to agree to marry me in such a hurry, did you?"

"No," she murmured, remembering how she had thought when she had first heard him speak that his was a voice she could fall in love with. He had, she thought, evaded her question quite neatly.

"I had imagined — or was I just being conceited when I finally persuaded you — that you had a small fondness for me that had nothing to do with the Merrick wealth or reputation, or am I wrong?"

"No, you're not wrong, dear Piers," she said, adding humbly, "I'm — I'm sorry for the terrible things I must have said to you. I'm sorry for making a scene."

She had thought she owed him that much, that by apologising for feminine weakness she would assure him that such an annoyance would not occur again, but the warmth which possibly she had only imagined seemed suddenly withdrawn.

"Never apologise," he said rather brusquely, "to me or

to Tibby or to anyone who shakes your self-confidence. The world takes one at face value, you see, and it doesn't do to be humble."

She felt reproved and puzzled at the same time. In her childhood humility had been considered a virtue and a conceit of one's own opinions a failing not to be encouraged. How, she wondered, did one assess one's own potentialities, and still remain oneself?

"You don't understand humility, do you?" she said tentatively, and he frowned.

"I don't like doormats," he replied with more curtness than he probably intended, and was surprised by the sudden glint in her eye.

"That," she remarked, "was rather uncalled for, and you've said it before. I'm no doormat for any man."

He had already got to his feet as if regretting his carelessly offered comfort, and he looked down at her with a hint of apology, observing the ruffled fringe which lent such an immature air to her face, but observing too the natural dignity which was often to be found in the very young.

"Yes, it was uncalled for," he said gently. "I apologise."

"You've just told me one should never apologise," she countered, aware now only of a desire for sleep, and he flicked back the teasing fringe with an exploratory finger.

"So I did. You're about all in, aren't you? I suggest you go straight to bed and leave unpacking till the morning."

"But it must be nearly dinner time. Miss Tibby will expect – "

"I'll have a tray sent up, and for heaven's sake don't address the old faggot as Miss Tibby – she'll only despise you the more," he said, but his impatience could hardly touch her now, for her eyelids were already heavy with exhaustion.

"Yes, of course . . ." she murmured, and barely heard the door close softly behind him.

She roused herself sufficiently to pick at the food which Tibby brought her later, but the old woman's regard was so contemptuous and at the same time so triumphant at this show of weakness in the bride that Lou made no effort to placate her.

When Piers came up after a solitary dinner made no easier by Tibby's thinly veiled satisfaction as she waited on him, he found the door between the two rooms had been left invitingly open, and the oil-lamp still burning, but Lou herself was asleep. She slept with the untroubled abandonment of a child, one arm flung above her head, and he stood there watching her for several minutes before he blew out the lamp and went quietly to his dressing-room.

To Lou those first days at Rune were a curious mixture of conflicting emotions. Even on the very first day she had been left alone. Piers had business on the mainland and would be back late, or possibly not until tomorrow, Tibby had told her with barely concealed malice. Lou, refreshed after a good night's sleep, and more prepared to meet the old woman's hostility, refused to allow dismay or disappointment to give her satisfaction. It was only polite, she thought that first morning, to propitiate and enlist Tibby's aid in finding her way about her new home, but the small sop was not appreciated.

"Go where you like, the place isn't big," Tibby said repressively. "There's no need for me to waste time showing you round."

Lou sighed, wishing she had not made the offer, but she was relieved all the same that she could explore the house alone. She had seldom had to deal with servants in the past, which might, she reflected, make her own approach awkward, but neither had she met with such unreasoning hostility. She wondered for the first time what the popular press had made out of the Merrick wedding which must have provided such a boundless source of copy for the gossip writers. Piers, if he had read the papers, had made no comment, but Tibby from her remarks last night clearly had. Cinderella stuff probably, thought Lou, remembering how fond Piers was of addressing her by that absurd name, and how careful Cousin Blanche would have been to keep Melissa out of the limelight in the circumstances.

Piers' house, Lou found with surprise, was unexpectedly simple, and his own adjectives immediately sprang to mind as she walked from room to room. Bare and monastic, he had said with faint mockery, and it was both. Plain rush matting covered most of the floors and passages, the walls were whitewashed and naked of pictures and the furniture comfortable but sparse. It was as if, thought Lou on what seemed to be a strange voyage of discovery into another's personality, Rune was not only a refuge, a small kingdom that might not be invaded, but an escape, perhaps, from the wealthy trappings to which nine-tenths of the year he must be accustomed. Only the main living-room had warmth and colour with its book-lined walls and the stone hearth piled with glowing peat and driftwood. Here, Lou supposed, they would spend their evenings, and here with lamplight and drawn curtains she would learn to know and perhaps love this dark stranger who was now her husband.

But that dream, she reflected later when he did not return, had been premature. She dined alone, waited on by the unsmiling Tibby, and sat alone through the long evening, wondering when the launch would make harbour, listening to the unfamiliar night sounds of the island, the sea and the gulls, the occasional hoot of a ship's siren, and her isolation seemed very complete.

"Best go to bed, missis," Tibby's dry voice said from the doorway. "He'll not be back tonight."

Lou started guiltily, aware that she had let the fire go down and the hour was past midnight.

"You shouldn't have waited up, Tibby," she said, trying to sound friendly. "I can lock up if you tell me where the different doors are."

The woman laughed with disagreeable scorn.

"Lock up on the island! We don't bother with those town practices here. Who do you think would row out from the mainland to burgle the house?" she replied. "As to waiting up, it was only on account of some jobs I had to finish. I never sit up for Mr. Piers – too unpredictable in his habits. If you come now, I'll light you up to bed. The lamps have been doused."

Lou, because she was clearly being a nuisance by lingering, followed the woman and her candle up the stairs, wondering a little at this belated act of courtesy, but when they reached her room and Tibby stood in the doorway watching her, she knew. The bed had not been moved in from the room next door.

For a moment Lou shrank from making any comment, but the woman stood there waiting, and there had to be a first time for establishing authority.

"Why haven't you had the other bed brought in, Tibby?" she asked quietly.

"There's been no time."

"There's been all day."

"The men were busy," Tibby said, referring to the two young islanders who helped about the house during the day.

It seemed strange to Lou to find young men doing the daily chores, but Tibby, Piers had said, would not tolerate another woman in the house.

"Well, please see that it's done in the morning," Lou said, remembering with slight discomfort the curious stare of the youth who had risen dutifully to his feet when she had entered the kitchen; Sam something or other, possessed of inordinate good looks and clearly Tibby's favourite. "Goodnight."

"Happen Mr. Piers will have changed his mind by

morning," Tibby said slyly. "Don't seem in a hurry to get on with his honeymooning, do 'e? Goodnight."

It was the first time she had spoken with any hint of the Cornish accent she must have picked up since coming to Rune, and as she closed the door, Lou shivered. It had cost her an effort to assert herself, and she had, after all, come out worst. If it was obvious, she thought, that Tibby had deliberately disregarded Piers' orders, the fact still remained that the bridegroom was in no haste to return to his bed and his newly wedded wife.

She slept restlessly, wondering how best to greet him when he did come back to her, how best to hide her chagrin that she seemed of such little account, but when morning came she found she had almost forgotten, and was only eager to explore the island. She asked Tibby to pack her a sandwich lunch and went joyfully out into the sunshine.

It did not take long to find her way down to the tiny natural harbour where boats lay bobbing lazily and nets were spread on the rocks to dry. A small shack did duty as a general store, selling mostly paraffin and tobacco and the emergency rations which might be required in times of storm, but the needs of the island must be small, for three cottages and the house appeared to be Rune's only habitations.

She spent the day clambering over rocks, discovering caves and pools and strange, unfamiliar shells along the shore. The weather had turned unusually mild for November and it was difficult to believe that storms could ever disturb the tranquil blue of the sea. The day was so still and so bright that the mainland looked very close, and cottages and traffic moving on the road above the cliffs could clearly be seen. Rune, Lou thought with surprise, only made a pretence of being isolated; a second motor launch had been moored in the harbour, and a couple of speedboats. How strange that the sophisticated and much publicised Piers Merrick should still be playing king-of-the-castle games, paying, it was said, a fantastic price for an unproductive little piece of land which he could claim as his realm; or was it, perhaps, his own private venture into makebelieve?

Diverted by a wider fissure in the rock face which looked like a passage, she saw out of the tail of her eye a launch approaching the island. It could be Piers returning, she supposed, and if she was quick she could meet him at the jetty. The passage, as it proved to be, however, was inviting and her curiosity aroused. Piers had left her without explanation her very first day on the island, so why should she hurry to welcome him back?

She squeezed gingerly through the aperture, feeling at once the chill and damp of subterraneous places, splashing through pools, stumbling over hidden rocks, experiencing a small tremor of fear at the darkness and the unknown hazards which might lie ahead. Suddenly the passage widened, a spear of light split the darkness and, standing in a pool of salt water, she blinked at the extraordinary cave which, like the transformation scene in a pantomime, had suddenly opened out before her. It was a cave which even her ignorance of such things could tell had been fashioned by man as well as by nature. A great slab of stone directly under the shaft of light gave the appearance of an altar, rough carvings had been hewn in the rock walls, and the roof towered in a natural sweep to the far distant opening to the sky from where the light was coming. Stalactites hung from the rock, catching the light with incredible beauty, so many of them that the place seemed alive with winking, reflected light, but the water below the altar, if altar it was, looked black and fathomless and the edges of the crater in which it lay seemed to have been crudely fashioned into some sort of semblance of a vast basin.

Lou felt an atavistic shiver pass through her as she stared down into the dark pool, and her wedding ring, so loose that it was always slipping off, slid over her cold finger and sank, with a tiny splash, beneath the evil-looking water.

For a moment she knew dismay, and a foreboding of ill fortune, then she remembered that the ring had been meant for Melissa and that ill fortune, if it came, should pass her by.

But the small mishap troubled her. The place seemed suddenly evil and the longing for sunlight and the familiar freshness of the open air drove her back down the passage. The cave was so beautiful, with its myriad facets of light, but she wanted to get away; she wanted the warmth of Piers' hearth, though empty of his presence, even of Tibby, who, insolent and resentful though she might be, was still flesh and blood and a formidable antidote to fanciful imaginings. But the passage seemed different. Coming, she had splashed through pools in the darkness, but now the water was continuous and noticeably higher. She had not reckoned, she realized in her city-bred ignorance, with tides and the menace of the sea; she had forgotten the stories she had heard of the disregarded dangers of the Cornish coast. The water seemed to be rising with alarming speed, rushing in through the passage with a spate of spume and spray, echoing from the rocks with an ominous boom.

Lou retreated, afraid that the rush of water would knock her down and drown her, but presently she started fighting her way back again; better to drown here quickly than in that sacrificial cave, climbing on to the altar stone for safety, but only prolonging the end while she watched the water rise. She thought, in her ignorance, that one of the storms of which Piers had warned her must have suddenly arisen while she explored the cave, and she emerged at last into the sunlight with a sense of shock. The sky was as blue, the sea as calm as before; only the diminishing stretch of sand had changed. The tide was coming in; in a very little while the water would have reached the mouth of the passage, blocking escape.

Lou turned to run with all speed back to the safety of the harbour and the cottages and found herself caught in a rough, ungentle grasp.

"What the hell do you think you're doing, spying and prying round my domain?" Piers' furious voice demanded, and for a moment she scarcely gathered the sense of his words, so relieved was she to find contact with human hands.

"I might have been drowned," she said in protest. "I found a passage in the rock and a wonderful cave – only I think it was evil. I – I don't know about tides, Piers. I suppose I should have asked."

"So you found the Druid's Cave, did you?" he said. "That was my own discovery when I first bought the island. How dare you go snooping without my sanction?"

"I might have been drowned," she said again, aware that he was extremely angry, but not, as she had first supposed, on account of anxiety for her.

"You were perfectly safe," he replied chillingly. "The cave never fills to danger point except in the storms."

"Oh!" She felt deflated and at the same time indignant at his unconcern.

"Have you no common sense?" he said, marching her resolutely along the shore. "Tides and currents can be dangerous in this part of the world, even though the cave is safe enough in this weather. You should have told Tibby where you were going"

"How did I know where I was going?" she retorted reasonably. "I was simply exploring – not snooping or prying, as you seem to think. Why shouldn't I, anyway?"

"Because," he said, "the island is mine, and I show it to whom I please. If you'd waited – "

She was about to counter that, as she had been deserted so early on their honeymoon, it hadn't seemed to her that he would care how she spent her time, but feeling his ungentle grip on her arm and glancing at his hard, implacable profile, she refrained, realizing that she had hurt him in some inexplicable fashion; that, like a small boy, he had planned to show her his treasures, and she had taken that pleasure from him and, more unforgivable still, had stumbled upon his own special discovery.

They walked to the house in silence, and Tibby, who must have been watching for them, observed with caustic pleasantry:

"Town clothes aren't fit for Rune. Made a pretty mess of your trousseau already, haven't you, missis?"

Lou glanced ruefully at the ruin of what had once been an elegant and costly creation. Melissa's smart wardrobe, she thought, had hardly been designed for a honeymoon such as this.

"I haven't anything else," she said, wondering if Tibby knew that all those unsuitable garments had not been intended for her.

"We'd better get you some slacks and jerseys, or something," Piers said absently, observing Lou's dishevelment without much interest. "Town-bred women seldom have anything suitable for roughing it, Tibby."

The woman made no comment, but her smile hinted plainly that his choice in brides was no less unsuitable.

"Where were you?" she asked Lou. "Mr. Piers was surprised not to find you here."

"She found the Druid's Cave. She seemed to think she might drown," Piers said, his voice tinged with ridicule.

"Oh," said Tibby. "Your special treasure – what a shame." Her sharp eyes went to Lou's twisting hands. "What's become of your wedding ring, missis?"

"It fell into the pool. It was too big," Lou said nervously, and the old woman smiled with a dark, secret knowledge, not only, thought Lou, because she must have known the ring had been made for another bride.

"Maybe you've made your peace-offering sacrifice,

maybe not," she said obscurely.

"Sacrifice?"

"The voice demands sacrifice, didn't you know? But then you were offering up what wasn't yours, so maybe it won't count."

"Tibby!" snapped Piers, the anger back in his voice. "Stop talking nonsense and take yourself off."

"I meant no harm," Tibby replied, and went away with a sly, backward smile at Piers.

"What did she mean about sacrifice – and the voice?" Lou asked, considerably shaken by the reception her harmless exploit had received from both of them.

"Superstitious nonsense she's picked up from the locals, I imagine. She was upset because you'd taken it upon yourself to explore without permission," he said, and Lou exclaimed with exasperation:

"Anyone would think I'd committed sacrilege the way you two go on about that stupid old cave! I thought it was horrible, anyway."

Only then did his eyes soften to amusement as if he remembered he must be tolerant of a child's blunders

"Then you're not likely to visit it again, are you?" he said. "Go and get cleaned up, Cinderella. Prince Charming would never look at you in that state."

She ran upstairs to change into another of Melissa's dresses, wondering if his remark was purely idle or was intended to convey a hint, but when they met again he appeared to be occupied with facts and figures concerning the business matter which had taken him to the mainland. He had meant nothing that should be taken seriously, evidently, thought Lou, but the Cinderella joke was wearing a bit thin.

She left him at last still juggling with figures, and began to make ready for bed. The day had, after all, ended badly. She had unwittingly trespassed in his private world, not waiting to be granted the freedom of his kingdom, and

Tibby, she was sure, had made more mischief, for despite her remarks last night, nobody had moved the second bed. For a moment she felt anger and a sense of defeat, but she could do nothing now. She remembered the old woman saying: "Happen Mr. Piers will have changed his mind by morning," and perhaps he had. Perhaps he already had regrets for his hasty marriage, or perhaps the car accident had shaken him up more than he would admit. In either event she could scarcely ask him, so, as a token that she understood, she closed the door firmly between their rooms and went to bed.

CHAPTER FIVE

But the next day Piers had become a different person. Lou, waking uneasily to the prospect of the long, uncertain hours ahead, found him standing by her bed with a tray of early morning tea and a quite humble request that he might share it with her. Sun poured in at the windows and the sky held the delicate promise of spring rather than of the approaching winter.

"How odd to think it's November," she said, remembering the wet greyness of her wedding day and the early twilight which seemed to descend so quickly upon London, "but Cornwall has a different climate, hasn't it?"

"So they say. This is probably a freak spell of halcyon weather before the storms set in," he replied. "We must make the most of it."

She glanced at him shyly, wondering if his remark contained more than an allusion to the weather, and he smiled back at her with reassurance, sitting on the side of the bed drinking his tea, bringing a comfortable warmth to the small shared intimacy.

"I'm sorry about yesterday," he said. "I didn't really mind you exploring the island, you know. I – I wanted to show it to you myself."

She released a little sign of pleasure. It was nice to know that for all his reputed wealth and sophistication, he was still young enough to care about a childish disappointment.

"I should have realized," she said. "It was just that I wanted something to fill the day. I'm sorry, too."

"You felt deserted, didn't you?"

"Not exactly, but – I wanted to get away from Tibby, I suppose. I'm afraid she doesn't like me."

"Tibby's just jealous – not only because she doesn't want

any competition here on Rune, but because she thought that in marrying Melissa I would cancel out a slight."

"A slight?"

"To my father, and so to her. She was prepared to put up with Blanche's daughter, you see, for she too fell under the old spell. Tibby's rather feudal in her ideas."

"You're a little feudal yourself," Lou said, wondering at the same time whether she was rash to submit a small challenge, but he only smiled.

"Yes, well . . . it's a habit you'll doubtless break me of in time, Cinderella," he replied, and watched with affectionate amusement the flash of surprise and doubt which came into her eyes. She looked so like a rather uncertain little girl sitting propped against her pillows, her face innocent of make-up, her hair soft and uncurled, ruffled from sleep like a child's, that he was, not for the first time, a little ashamed of the ease with which he had acquired an unwilling bride.

"Were you unwilling?" he asked, adding as he saw her forehead wrinkle in perplexity under the disordered fringe, "I was following my own thoughts. I was referring to unwilling brides."

He spoke too lightly for her to be sure whether he meant to be taken seriously, and she was as yet too inexperienced to retaliate provocatively and keep him guessing.

"You must know I wasn't," she answered with simple honesty. "I would never have married you, even for Cousin Blanche's sake, if I hadn't – if I hadn't – "

"If you hadn't what?"

But she could not, in the face of such an unpropitious start to a honeymoon, embarrass him with further offers of compliance. She could not tell him that the attraction he held for her might, with such little effort on his part, turn so easily to love. She did not even know, if in spite of his earlier warnings, he meant to demand anything of her at all.

"If I hadn't liked you, of course," she answered primly, and thought he put down his empty cup and got to his feet with a certain air of relief.

"Of course," he echoed with a tinge of mockery. "Well, get up and get dressed now, lazybones. The day's too good to waste indoors. Tibby can put us up a picnic and we'll do a tour of inspection."

It was the first of many such days. The unseasonable weather continued to hold, deceiving Lou into imagining that this remote little island was not only cut off from the outside world's demands, but from the vagaries of the elements as well. As she came to know the island, she came also to know a little of Piers, and realized she had been right when she had told her cousin that Rune was, for him, an escape. He seemed relaxed and at ease in this wild solitude and his tongue lost its sharp arrogance as he patiently explained island customs and answered questions. Lou was grateful to him for sharing his small kingdom with her and careful never to trespass with proposals of her own.

Once he said to her: "You look at me sometimes, Lou, as if you didn't understand. You don't, do you?"

She shook her head dumbly. She had such little self-conceit that she accepted his apparent reluctance to consummate their marriage as a sign of regret for his hasty action, just as she accepted Tibby's prevarications about moving the second bed. She knew, and Tibby knew, that the excuse of the car accident had served its purpose; the stitches had been taken out, the scar was nearly healed, and there was nothing left to suppose but that the accident had been a timely let-out for Piers.

"No, you don't understand," he said, breaking into her thoughts with a certain roughness. "Why do you imagine I brought you to the island?"

They were on the shore and he had pinioned her gently but firmly against the rock face with one of those sudden changes of mood she found so disconcerting.

"Because it was easiest, I suppose," she answered, groping vainly for the right words. "I mean the – the honeymoon you had planned would have been – would have been – "

"Wasted, were you going to say?" he mocked as she broke off uncertainly. "Oh, no, my dear, that honeymoon was devised for obvious reasons – the sort of tour-de-luxe expected in the circumstances. On the island one has a chance to get to know one another."

She blinked up at him, the wind stinging her eyes to an impression of tears which she brushed away impatiently.

"But surely you would have wanted to get to know Melissa?" she said gently, and his slow grin was both confusing and a little alarming.

"I already knew all that was necessary about Melissa, and I don't think she was proposing to dig much below the surface where I was concerned," he said, and she experienced a small, irrational spurt of anger.

"If you were both so indifferent to each other, then I'm not surprised she ran off with someone else," she retorted, and his smile became suddenly tender.

"You'd never seize an advantage where you could, would you?" he said with amusement. "Most girls would be rubbing it in how badly I'd been treated."

"Perhaps I don't think you have been badly treated," she replied, standing her ground. "If Melissa knew you were simply making what you thought to be a suitable marriage, you can hardly complain if she preferred someone else at the last moment."

"Oh, I'm not complaining. Still, I wouldn't like you to think I'm entirely devoid of natural feelings. I wasn't indifferent to Melissa in the sense you imply. She's a very attractive young woman," he said deliberately, and knowing that he had hurt her, took a perverse pleasure in watching her instant recoil.

"Of course," she said. "I spoke without thinking, I suppose. All the same, it was hardly fair to marry me out of spite, was it?"

Anger, to which he knew he had no right, suddenly possessed him. She looked so slight and fragile imprisoned by his outstretched hands against the rock face that he experienced a savage desire to shake her, beat her even, for exposing an imagined weakness in him.

"You pay too much attention to Tibby's unflattering views," he replied, speaking with the old cold arrogance because he refused to allow temper to reduce him to a childish display of violence, but he still had not learnt that for all her unsureness there was the courage of a small trapped animal in Lou.

"Tibby only says what all the world must think," she retorted. "That's why you brought me here to Rune, isn't it – to hide me away until people have stopped laughing?"

His arms fell to his sides, releasing her had she wished to turn and run, but when she did not move, his hands moved out again to touch her tentatively, to draw her against him with gentleness, to wait with humility while her young body, denying the bitterness of her words, yielded unprotestingly to his.

"Try to bear with me, Lou," he said, and did not know how easily his voice could work its old charm with her. "I'll admit that there could be a certain amount of truth in the reasons my friends will doubtless put about, but that was yesterday. People can change their reasons in a day, in an hour, and I brought you to Rune, not to hide you away from the gossip and laughter, but to hide us both until we had become acquainted. I thought I had made that clear when I answered your original question."

"Nothing's very clear, Piers," she said, and found she was weeping.

"Now look what I've done," he said, wiping away the tears with a careful finger. "You mustn't take me too seriously, Cinderella, when I give way to moods. I don't understand myself half the time."

"That's my difficulty – to know."

"To know?"

"When to take you seriously, and when not. I – I have such very little experience of men."

"What, no admirers? No would-be suitors?"

He was, she guessed, lightly teasing to tide them both over embarrassment, but she answered with her usual naïve truthfulness:

"One or two admirers, perhaps – office Lotharios bored with their wives. Suitors weren't so easily come by; young men starting to earn a living these days haven't much money."

"How charming you are, how refreshingly unfeminine," he said, surprised that he should feel such annoyance at the thought of the office Lotharios, but realized at once that he had phrased things badly.

"Unfeminine?" she repeated, drawing away from him, but he pulled her back again and kissed the tip of her nose.

"Not in the sense you've taken it, silly goose," he laughed. "Perhaps I should have said un-bitchy. Now let's go home and see what Tibby has for tea."

All the way back along the wet sands, he charmed her with anecdotes and an occasional implied compliment, lifting her over the deeper pools with uncharacteristic consideration for her comfort, behaving, thought the inexperienced Lou, with the rather surprising concern of a lover.

Piers watched with a certain wryness as, the harbour and house in sight, she sped away from him with the careless abandon of a child released from adult supervision. She was too young, too unpractised, he supposed, to understand that he had begun his wooing. He might have married her out of hand for any or all of the reasons attributed to him, but he would not claim any rights until he could offer a little of the courtship of which he had cheated her.

A week or more went by with still no break in the phenomenal weather, It was, thought Lou, ready as always to marvel at and accept the extraordinary, as if the very seasons conspired to perpetuate her fairy tale. The sun and the breeze had the gentle freshness of the spring of the year and it was warm enough to wander without coats and picnic in the shelter of the rocks.

Out of doors Lou remained unquestioningly happy, learning to adapt herself to Piers' moods, his teasing and casual probing, his long silences, even the sharpness of the tongue he could not always control.

For him, too, the days brought bounty and the new fascination of exploring another's personality, and, so skilful was he, Lou seldom realized how much of herself she revealed to him. But she did know that when they returned to the house, they seemed to slip back into becoming strangers again and the evenings would seem long and filled with uneasy silences or, worse, the angry squabbles which flared up between Piers and Tibby. She knew that their bickering was habitual rather than deliberate, but every so often the old woman would presume too much, or Piers' casual rudeness would strike a bitter note and the quarrel would become unendurable to one unable to listen to harshness without pain. So often, too, Piers' irritation would swing to Lou because her shrinking apprehension of such scenes riled him much more than Tibby's accustomed gibes and because, too, he imagined that shrinking sprang from other causes. She was, perhaps, dreading the moment when the evening ended, and she might find on going upstairs that he had had the second bed moved into her room. Well, that day would come, whether she liked it or not, he would think to himself a little grimly, but not yet; not until the time was ripe and the foolish child had ceased to stare at him across the dinner table with such blank, accusing eyes.

Lou, except for the rather galling fact that he clearly

seemed to have no use for her as a woman, was less concerned about the position of the bed than he, had he but known it. Her common sense told her that Tibby was jealous, and the hints and innuendoes she dropped when Piers was not around sprang mainly from a desire to show displeasure at her nursling's unsuitable choice of a bride. She would, doubtless, have been jealous of Melissa, but at least Melissa would have been acceptable in that she was Blanche Chailey's daughter.

Lou, as the days went by, wished she could learn the way to Tibby's tolerance as easily as Sam Smale, that handsome young fisherman who spoke little and hardly at all to Lou, but who was plainly the apple of Tibby's eye.

"You're fond of Sam, aren't you?" she once said, hoping to find some common ground on which they might meet, and for a moment the old servant's expression softened to something approaching affection.

"He's a good lad. A mite proud of his looks, maybe, but a good lad," she said. "When Mr. Piers is away on his pleasures there's no one much to worry about."

"Do you worry about Piers still?" Lou asked shyly, thinking that perhaps she had found the key, only to be driven back behind her own frail defences at the withering look she received.

"Worry about him!" Tibby scoffed, but there was a trace of contemptuous pity in her hard eyes. "What should the likes of him need of a woman's comfort when money can buy anything, even love?"

"I don't think that's true."

"Isn't it? You married him, didn't you, for all he was pledged to another? Would you have taken him so quickly without the Merrick wealth?"

"Yes – yes, I think I would."

"More fool you, then. Don't think, young missis, that because that other one threw him over he's forgotten her. Men do daft things for injured pride and live to regret it.

Is she like her mother?"

"Yes, very," Lou replied shortly. It was not pleasant to glimpse the possible truth through the rosy mists of make-believe.

"Then you made a bad mistake taking him from her," Tibby snapped. "Didn't I warn you when you found the cave?"

"You dropped vague hints about voices and sacrifices, but Piers says that's a lot of superstitition," Lou answered more sharply than she intended, for she was becoming impatient with this perpetual belittling, but the old woman merely looked smug and a little sly.

"Because he'll not want to remember the legend so soon. Happen he's sorry already he's put you in another's place. He'd never have brought her here, that's for sure," she said, and suddenly leaned towards Lou with confidential avidity.

"What was she like, Miss Blanche's girl?" she asked, but Lou could not tell her.

What was Melissa like? she wondered, going away to speculate in private. She had, she supposed, never known the real Melissa behind that smart, sparkling façade, had thought, indeed, that there might not be much to know should the glamour and the fashionable little tricks and provocations be stripped away, but even so, Melissa had thrown away a brilliant match for love, so after all she was vulnerable, and Lou, already halfway in love herself, thought humbly of the cousin who had made her own good fortune possible. She hoped most sincerely that she was happy, wondering, with the first stirrings of curiosity, what sort of man had supplanted Piers so easily.

"Who is he – this man Melissa ran off with?" she asked him later that day, then wished she had not as she saw the hardness settle in his face.

"Some minor scion of the stage, so I understand. I never met him," he answered curtly.

"I shouldn't have asked you, perhaps?"

"Why not? You have a right to your natural curiosity."

"It wasn't curiosity in the vulgar sense."

"And what do you suppose you mean by that? All curiosity is vulgar. One's private failures – and their opposite – should be allowed decent burial."

He spoke with a definite edge to his voice, and she flushed and lowered her eyes. He was warning her, she supposed, not to trespass, reminding her, possibly, that she was still the Cinderella of the story and, as such, must be grateful for Prince Charming's benefice without probing his innermost thoughts too deeply.

She sighed without realizing the soft, sad little sound could reach him, and he cocked an eyebrow at her.

"Don't cry for the moon, Cinderella – it's only made of green cheese," he observed cryptically, and she thought again he was warning her not to expect too much of him.

"I expect nothing," she said aloud, forgetting that he had no means of reading her thoughts, and Tibby's acid voice spoke from the doorway.

"Very sensible, missis. Those that expect nothing won't be disappointed," she said, and placed a lighted oil-lamp on the table.

It was a trick of Tibby's, Lou had learnt, coming soft-footed into the room and remaining to add her own contribution to the conversation. Lou thought that the old woman often listened outside the door before entering, since her remarks were usually apt and uncomfortable.

"That's a very defeatist point of view, Tibby," Piers observed, apparently restored to good humour. "And no consolation to a bride, would you say?"

"When you don't see fit to take your bride to your bed there's little enough for the poor maid to expect," Tibby retorted, and Lou jumped as Piers' fist came crashing down on the arm of his chair.

"That's enough!" he snapped. "If you can't keep your

bawdy thoughts to yourself you'd best stay silent. Get out, and don't interrupt us again till dinner time.''

Lou would have liked to escape in Tibby's wake. Instead she slid to the floor by the fire to hide her burning cheeks from him. The room, she thought, with firelight warm on the book-lined walls, and the intimate clutter of everyday life forming a pattern of comfortable domesticity, should have felt safe and familiar and been a pleasant refuge to return to after a day in the open, but she had come to dread the four walls which enclosed them in uneasy companionship, the sense of trespass which Tibby and, sometimes, Piers himself, imposed upon her.

"I apologise for Tibby. I've allowed her too much freedom of speech in the past," Piers said, then, as she did not speak, he leaned forward and twisted her round to face him.

"You don't know what to think, do you, Lou?" he asked with unembarrassed amusement, then as he saw the mute enquiry in her wide-set eyes, his face changed again.

"Poor Cinderella," he said, his voice rough and a little mocking. "Do you think I don't know? Night after night you wonder, don't you? And night after night you breathe a sigh of relief as you climb into your solitary bed."

The bright colour had faded, but she met his eyes without evasion.

"You know nothing about my inner thoughts," she replied with composure. "And if you've been watching me night after night with mistaken notions, you've only yourself to blame."

"Dear me!" he said, momentarily nonplussed as he sometimes was by the unexpected directness of attack. "For all that, my dear, you were distinctly relieved when my crack on the head coincided with our wedding night, weren't you? Very natural, I hasten to add, since I was a comparative stranger to you."

"Yes, you were a stranger," she said, and might have

added more had he not spoken so lightly with the half-impatient indulgence one would throw to a child. With her thoughts so recently full of Melissa it was not difficult to understand that he abstained from the privileges of marriage because, when it came to the point, substitution was no satisfactory exchange for the real thing.

"Piers – " she said at last, " – why do you suppose I married you?"

From his expression he had clearly expected the question to be put the other way.

"Glamour . . . story-book stuff . . ." he answered carelessly. "Besides, we bullied you into it, Blanche and I."

"Yes, it was story-book stuff. It still is in a sort of way – the island, the unnatural weather, Tibby like the Bad Fairy laying curses instead of gifts, and you – "

"And I, I suppose, am the Demon King, or is it the Demon Lover? What a child you are!"

"You are not a lover at all, and I am no child," she said, and he leaned forward again and pulled her roughly against his knee.

"You're a child to me in comparison to such ladies who have seen fit to be kind to me," he said, but the raillery had gone from his voice now and she reached up a hand to touch his face.

"You must try to forget my lack of experience," she said gently. "I so often don't know how to take you."

"Poor Cinderella . . . I haven't really been fair, have I?"

"Even Cinderella stepped out of the cinders, and as far as we're told, lived happily ever after with her prince."

"And this prince is hardly doing his stuff, you're thinking?"

She rubbed her cheek against his knee, wishing he would not talk to her as if she were a child, though perhaps that was his only defence against an embarrassing situation. He felt the little quiver of protest that ran through her body, and turned her face up to his.

"Forgive me if I seem to talk down to you," he said with that odd flash of perception that so often took her by surprise. "And try to remember that I'm adjusting the balance."

"What do you mean?"

"Well, I put the cart before the horse by my fine gesture, didn't I? I married you without any courtship, which I believe is important to a girl, so we must start again. Do you understand, now?"

Her face became suddenly so radiant that he wondered for a brief moment whether his policy of forbearance had been mistaken.

"In my own way – in my own time, we'll come to that happy ending," he said, and gently kissed her.

For Lou it was both a promise and an explanation. She thought of those carefree days in the open, remembering with impatience at her own stupidity, the half-tender approaches, the gentle teasing which she had dismissed so lightly because she had thought he was merely being kind. He had, after all, been trying to pave the way to a deeper relationship and, whatever his regrets for his hasty action, he was prepared to stand by it with unlooked-for consideration. *In my own way ... in my own time ...* he had said, and the evenings were no longer an awkward hiatus between the day and the morrow, and even Tibby's barbs could be smiled at and forgotten.

"You'm proper pleased with yourself, all of a sudden, bain't you?" the old woman said, after one of her more acid remarks had met with no reaction, and Lou knew from the fact that Tibby had unconsciously slipped into the Cornish idiom that she was more than ordinarily disturbed.

"Why should you mind if I'm pleased with myself, Tibby?" Lou asked, trying for the first time to win the antagonistic old woman over to toleration if not to liking.

"Honeymoons are times for self-congratulation, wouldn't you say?" She spoke deliberately, proffering a challenge because, in her new-found felicity, she was no longer afraid of Tibby.

The woman observed her narrowly, recognising a change which she could not account for but knowing at the same time that she could, if she chose, soon prick this little bubble of complacency.

"Honeymoons is for lovers," she stated repressively. "The way you were wed, missis, hardly calls for joy bells."

"You are rather impertinent," Lou said quietly, stung at last to an assertion of authority, and was surprised to find the method worked. Tibby's thin lips compressed and her eyes narrowed, but when she next spoke it was with the artificial voice of a well-trained servant.

"I beg pardon, madam," she said. "Will you be wanting anything special for dinner?"

It was so out of character that Lou laughed and knew at once that she had immediately lost ground, if indeed, any had been gained. Tibby raised her sparse, almost non-existent eyebrows in contemptuous reproof and observed, still in that correct, but somehow insolent voice:

"I'm only waiting for orders."

"You know very well that my wishes are of no account. Running the house and ordering the meals are your province. It wouldn't please you now if I were to ask for something for dinner that you hadn't already prepared, now would it?" Lou said, but she sighed as the woman left the room with a smirk of satisfaction. It was no good calling Tibby's bluff, for she would always have the last word. It was no good, either, striving to ingratiate herself by offers of help in the kitchen, or pleas for instruction in house-keeping, for this she had already tried with no success.

"Why the hell do you bother?" Piers had said impatiently when she confessed to failure. "Tibby resents interference, and I should have thought you would have been glad to be relieved of household chores."

"Most women like to feel they have a say in the matter of running their homes," she had replied without thinking and, although he said nothing, his raised eyebrows and the small twisted smile had told her plainly enough that, although he had married her, she was still a guest in his house.

Piers went occasionally to the mainland on unspecified business, but he did not take her with him. She knew vaguely that he owned property there as he did in many parts of the country, but he never discussed his business affairs with her and it was a long time before she knew of the many charitable boards on which he sat.

"Piers Merrick is a strange mixture," someone told her much later. "He doesn't mind his name being bandied about as a rich playboy or an idle young rake with a long and probably erroneous list of short-lived affairs, but let the press get hold of something worthwhile he does with his money and he's hopping mad."

But even early on Lou became aware of this contradiction in him. He would talk at length and amusingly about the lavish expenditure of his bachelor days, but when she discovered by chance the benefits reaped by charities and indigent friends, he shut up like a clam.

"Why do you like to be thought just rich and raffish and God's gift to the gossip columns?" she asked him once, and his eyebrows went up at such unaccustomed plain speaking from her.

"One gets labelled," he replied with lazy evasiveness. "And one should never disappoint one's public."

"Stuff and nonsense!" she exclaimed, sounding, he thought with amusement, oddly like Lewis Carroll's immortal Alice. "That's all right for film stars and publicity hunters, but not for a man."

"You really *are* like Alice at times. I'd never realized," he said with interest, and was delighted when she innocently enquired if Alice was one of his ex-girl-friends. But for all her hints, he still seemed reluctant to take her with him to the mainland, neither would he agree to a second visit to the Druid's Cave.

"Why not?" she asked. "I want to explore it properly."

"You didn't like the cave. You said it was evil."

"Yes, well ... I was scared that time. I wouldn't mind with you. Besides, Tibby says – "

"Tibby talks a great deal of nonsense if you're silly enough to listen," he said a little roughly.

"But there is a legend, isn't there?"

"Very likely. Cornwall is full of legends and superstitions. Leave the cave alone, Lou."

She submitted without argument, but her curiosity was aroused. One day, she thought, she would visit the cave again. In the meantime, her immediate needs were more pressing. Melissa's expensive trousseau was fast becoming ruined, and when Piers demanded somewhat impatiently to know why she did not wear more sensible clothes for messing about among rocks and pools, she replied with some indignation:

"Because there's nothing else. You said you would buy me slacks and jerseys, but you'll never take me to the mainland. Do you think I enjoy wearing Melissa's expensive things?"

"Melissa?"

"You must know that everything I have here was meant for her, and wasn't planned for this sort of life, anyway. There was no time to fit me out, besides – "

Besides, she had been going to say, *you were paying for it all*, but she broke off, watching the irritable frown which drove two deep furrows between his eyes, and knew that he had probably never given a thought to her wardrobe except to deplore her taste.

"Besides, it's time I bought you a wedding ring of your

own, you were going to say, weren't you?" he said with a change of manner. "You're quite right, of course. Tomorrow we'll go to Truro and remedy my neglect. I've been selfish wanting to keep you unspoilt on the island."

"Have you, Piers? Why?" she asked with surprise, and he grinned with a trace of sheepishness.

"Part of your fairy tale's rubbed off on me, perhaps, I'd a notion to keep you just for myself."

"That," she retorted with faint severity, "is rather absurd. You can hardly think of yourself as the jealous lover."

"Can't I? Well, perhaps not. Still, it's as well to lie fallow till all the excitement and gossip is forgotten, wouldn't you say?"

"That makes more sense. Will there have been much gossip?"

"What do you think? People have short memories, however. By the time I'm ready, curiosity will be dead. In the meantime I at least owe you a respectable wedding ring and a few essentials to personal comfort. Tomorrow we'll go on a shopping spree."

She had thought when the morrow came he would most likely have changed his mind, but he seemed in a festive mood, and if, at times, Lou felt rather like a schoolgirl being treated to an unexpected outing by an indulgent uncle, the day was a success. Shops were painstakingly explored for garments more suited to life on the island, a wedding ring bought, and some charming trinkets to go with it, and he observed with a slightly sardonic eye her simple pleasure in these trifles.

"I must take you back to London sooner or later," he said. "You'll need some decent jewellery, clothes of your own choosing. When we've done with Rune you'll be ready for more sophisticated pleasures. It will be rather fun to spoil you."

"How do you mean – done with Rune?"

"When it's served its purpose for our better acquaintance.

You haven't forgotten what I told you, have you?"

She had not, but she thought he might have. The Piers Merrick of popular conception was given to careless assurances, she knew.

"In your own way ... in your own time, you said," she replied a little shyly.

"Yes, Lou, just that. Bear with me for a while longer, will you?"

She smiled at him but made no answer. If he was renewing a promise or merely apologising for a lack of ardour, she did not wish to know then. The day had been so delightful and his consideration so gentle that she was content to fall in with whatever he might have in mind for them both, and by the time they started back in the launch for the island she knew his mood had changed again. Before leaving the town he had, on a sudden impulse, filled the car with flowers and fruit and extravagant baskets of hothouse blooms that would scarcely last a day divorced from their careful packing.

Lou gazed, wide-eyed, at the great colourful heap he had flung so carelessly into the boat, and then stole a look at his dark, impatient face as he took the helm. He glanced down at her at the same moment, and his smile was tender and a little amused.

"Were you thinking this display had rather a bridal air?" he asked, but her reply was lost on the wind.

"And why not?" he said enigmatically. "Perhaps we have waited too long."

When they reached harbour he lifted her on to the jetty, holding her for a moment against him before setting her down. So perfect was this delicate promise of fulfilment that even when one of the fishermen remarked that the weather was on the change, she refused to believe that anything could spoil the halcyon day.

"Oh, surely not!" she exclaimed, her eyes on the calm sea and cloudless sky, but Piers, pausing to sniff the wind, said the man was a good weather prophet and was probably right.

They walked up to the house, flowers strewing in their wake because there were too many to manage in one armful. She wanted to stop and pick them up, unwilling to leave them there to die, but Piers seemed impatient to get to the house.

"You won't miss them. What are a few flowers, anyway?" he said with the careless indifference of a man who could afford to buy up an entire florist's shop and replace them if necessary on the morrow.

"Shall you mind if the storms come?" he asked, sounding gay and a little provocative. "We might find ourselves cut off, you know."

He did not speak very seriously, but his eyes were suddenly a little anxious, and her heart lifted. To be cut off from the mainland with a husband at last embracing the mood of a lover could only be a blessing and a delight.

"No, Piers, I shan't mind at all," she replied with polite restraint, but her voice was as gay as his and she could laugh with real amusement at Tibby coming to meet them with a nursery air of outrage at the evidence of such wanton extravagance.

"What game are you playing now, Piers, I should like to know?" she demanded. " 'Tes carrying makebelieve too far to go squandering good money on lovers' nonsense. Rune's no place for fancy frills."

"The money happens to be mine, and the makebelieve is possibly yours, and my wife's entitled to as many fancy frills as she may desire," Piers retorted, and the old woman's suspicious glance went swiftly from him to Lou, quick to register the subtle change in both of them.

"If you're laying in for a siege, it would have been better to have bought supplies. Weather's on the change, they say," Tibby sniffed, but Lou noticed that for all her scorn, the woman's bleak eyes softened in spite of herself as they rested on the glowing pile of colour heaped on the stone flags.

"I'll arrange a special bowl of the best ones for your kitchen," Lou said, and saw, for the first time, an unwilling flash of pleasure in the woman's face before, with another sniff, she retired to the kitchen quarters from where smells of baking bread and toasting scones had wafted invitingly before the dividing door was closed. It was the hour for tea and relaxation before the evening began, and, despite the familiar antagonism which Tibby, and even the bare, monastic house exuded, Lou felt she had come home.

She ran upstairs to change her dress, aware that the day held a new significance, that she must meet her husband more than halfway, and, holding fast to this strange new thread which had been woven between them, match his demands with hers. After tea she would arrange her flowers, decking all the rooms with colour and gaiety, piling the fruit in glowing pyramids, abandoning herself to the hitherto unknown luxury of such abundance and the promise it surely contained.

Piers sat watching her at this occupation when, the tea-things cleared away, she darted in and out of the rooms with bowls and vases and every receptacle she could lay hands on. He thought how charming she looked with her soft hair flying and her skirts twirling as she sped with such earnest concentration from one flower arrangement to another. It was, he reflected with unfamiliar humility, a little chastening to discover how much delight could be given by so careless an impulse.

"Lou – come here," he said aloud, and at the odd urgency in his voice she dropped the flowers she held in her hands and ran across the room to him.

"What is it?" she asked, and was aware when he did not immediately reply that the wind was rising. It was rather pleasant, she thought inconsequentially, to become acquainted again with the proper seasons of the year, after the freakish calm of those days and nights on the island.

"What do you really think of me?" he asked unexpectedly, pulling her down to perch on the arm of his chair, and she stiffened uneasily, conscious that the wrong answer could wreck that new-found felicity between them.

"I – I don't know you very well yet," she temporised warily. "We're – only acquaintances still, aren't we?"

His arm tightened about her waist.

"Yes, my honest Lou, we're only acquaintances. We must remedy that, mustn't we?" he said.

"I don't always know how," she said simply, so afraid that she might be found wanting, and he looked up at her with an expression of tender apology.

"No, of course you don't," he said. "It should be my job to break down barriers."

"Some went today, don't you think?"

"Yes, I think so. But you make me feel ashamed that such treats can please you. I shall so enjoy taking you on a real shopping spree – buying you diamonds, furs – all the extravagant fripperies that women dream about. That's the only real pleasure money brings."

"I don't think I've ever coveted diamonds, and I have furs, although they weren't really meant for me," she replied with her usual considered truthfulness, and he laughed.

"Melissa's cast-offs have rankled, haven't they?"

"Not really – besides, they're all new and terribly expensive. It's just that – well, I felt I wasn't me any more."

"Poor Cinderella – that was thoughtless of me, wasn't it? Never mind, that can all be put right later. In the meantime you can wear those rather fetching slacks and whatnot we found today and discover yourself again. Kiss me, Lou. I don't think you ever have of your own accord."

"You don't do much kissing yourself, come to that," she observed prosaically, but she leaned over him obediently, and as her lips touched his she experienced an unselfconscious desire to explore, and dropped light caresses on his eyelids, his cheekbones, the sharp ridge of his nose, until he pulled her down into his arms and held her close.

She lay there contentedly after her pulses had ceased to race so wildly, and stared drowsily over his shoulder to the darkness outside the uncurtained windows. The familiar lights from the harbour cottages showed palely, a brighter, moving beam flashed on the water, and she caught the faint sound of an engine.

"There's a launch putting in to the harbour," she said idly.

"Extra supplies of booze in case the weather turns nasty, most likely," he replied, and relinquished her reluctantly as she remembered her forgotten flowers and struggled out of his arms.

Presently he left her to it and repaired to his study for an hour's paper work before dinner. Tomorrow, he thought with a smile, that bed should be moved to where it properly belonged, and tonight – well, a dividing door without a lock presented no difficulties.

Lou, finishing the last of her flower arrangements, was startled by the clamour of the ship's bell which hung by the front door. So seldom was it rung, since no one visited the island, that she experienced an irrational moment of superstitious dread. It was no ghost, however, tolling for admission. Tibby's footsteps could be heard, the rush of wind as the door opened, and the sound of voices. Presently confused steps returned across the hall, then Tibby's voice, harsh and somehow triumphant, announced from the doorway: "A visitor for 'ee, missis. I'd best prepare one of the guest rooms."

She stood aside, and Lou stared in disbelief at the newcomer who pushed confidently past the old servant.

"*Melissa!* What on earth are you doing here?" she exclaimed, and her cousin, stepping delicately across the room, bringing with her the familiar expensive little waft of her favourite scent, offered an unaccustomed embrace and observed with characteristic candour:

"God, what an outlandish dump! You must be quite crackers, Lou, to agree to such an uncivilised honeymoon, but perhaps you weren't asked. No, in view of everything, I suppose you hadn't much choice. Darling, I know it's madly tactless of me to come at such a time, but you will give me sanctuary, won't you? I'm in dire trouble – but *dire*, my dear."

Lou, too taken by surprise to formulate any coherent ideas, simply stared at her and murmured: "Of course . . ." in a vague, uncomprehending tone of voice, but Tibby, who had remained listening and watching, came forward now and looked Melissa over with a slow, careful air of assessment.

"You'm like your mother. You might even *be* Miss Blanche as I used to know her," she said, and Lou heard the slightly malicious pleasure in her voice, and knew with a sinking heart that despite her aversion to any feminine competition in the house she would be subservient to Melissa, if only to use her as a whipping-post.

"I'd best tell the master," she said with a sly, satisfied look at Lou, but at that moment Piers came into the room.

"Who rang the bell?" he asked, and as his eyes fell on Melissa, his whole frame stiffened visibly and his face froze into hardness.

"*Well* . . ." he said softly, and Lou knew that however she had dreamed the day would end, she was right back where she had started.

CHAPTER SIX

AFTERWARDS Lou did not know quite what she had expected. Piers said with blunt inhospitality:

"What are you doing here?"

Melissa replied with equal bluntness: "Blanche has turned me out."

"Blanche? But haven't you a husband now – or at least a – a protector?" Lou stammered, at the same time feeling foolish.

"What an old-fashioned expression," Piers interjected absently.

"No," Melissa said and, most uncharacteristically, began to cry.

Lou could not remember having seen her cousin in tears before, and the sight unnerved her. Melissa, of course, wept beautifully and without disfigurement, but her tears seemed real enough, and she did not, as might have been expected, turn to Piers for comfort, but to Lou.

"Darling, be generous," she sobbed. "You have so much, and I – well, I've been a fool."

"What's happened?" asked Lou, bewildered, and unsure of the right approach with Piers and Tibby standing there watching them both with such odd expressions.

"It's a long story and not very edifying – but don't turn me away, Lou. I've nowhere else to go," Melissa said, and Lou replied gravely:

"It's Piers' house, but I'm sure if you're in trouble – "

"Why should he care any more?" Melissa interrupted bitterly. "He married you, didn't he, without turning a hair? Tell him to go away, Lou, while I try to make you understand. You should feel sorry for me – and grateful, too, as things have turned out."

"Just like Miss Blanche all over again," Tibby murmured from the doorway, and Piers threw her an angry look.

"Get back to the kitchen, Tibby, and don't trade on old privileges," he snapped, but although the old woman turned obediently to leave the room, her smile was undefeated by sharp words.

"I'd best prepare one of the bedrooms first. Whatever your feelings, Mr. Piers, you can't send the young lady back before morning," she said, and went away.

Piers turned back into the room and stood for a moment regarding both girls with frowning impatience, his head thrust forward, his hands plunged in his pockets. A lamp flared in the draught of the closing door, lending his features a predatory look, and Lou shivered.

"I can do no less than offer you hospitality for the night, I suppose," he said at last, turning to Melissa. "And your story had better be good."

"Piers – " said Lou quickly, aware that the tender companion of the afternoon had vanished and that although he spoke harshly, his eyes rested on Melissa with that familiar look of speculation and appraisal.

"Yes?" For a moment his attention was diverted back to her, but his voice held only cool politeness as if it was she who was the stranger.

"Let me talk to Melissa alone. I don't think – well, I'm not sure – " Lou stumbled over the words and broke off a little helplessly, and he gave her a dark, rather cynical look.

"You're not sure of anything, my poor Cinderella, are you?" he said, and went out of the room.

Melissa dabbed at her wet lashes and then smiled her familiar dazzling smile.

"Is that what he calls you? And, of course, it's true, isn't it?" she said, but did not quite regain her composure under her cousin's grave, direct gaze.

"Quite true," Lou replied quietly, "but you have

only yourself to thank. As you've already pointed out, I should be grateful to you, and generous, so let's hear your story."

Melissa gave her a puzzled glance, but she altered her tone as if she appreciated that their positions were reversed, that by her own folly she had become the suppliant and not the careless dispenser of favours. Her story when told was, Lou supposed, common enough, but not the sort of situation in which the Melissas of this world might expect to find themselves. That old affair which Cousin Blanche had thought forgotten had, it seemed, been kept alive by sheer perversity on Melissa's part. It had relieved boredom when the first novelty of her engagement had worn off, she said; she had never meant things to go so far, but then the man had threatened disclosure, hinted at suicide, and she had lost her head.

"Did you believe him?" Lou asked, who found it hard to visualise her hard-boiled cousin either losing her head or being taken in, and Melissa began to cry again.

"I don't know – but it was flattering and – and I think I wanted to shake Piers up."

"Then you did care?"

"Yes, I suppose I did."

"And yet you ran away with someone else! Didn't you mean to marry him, then – this other man?"

"Of course not!"

"Then why did you do it?"

"I did it for kicks."

"For *kicks*?"

"Don't sound so outraged, darling, one does so many things for kicks. Life becomes boring when everything's too cut and dried. I thought I could show Piers that he wasn't getting me so easily. He's very spoilt, you know. I naturally never thought he wouldn't try to find me – that he would marry just any little ninny to save his face."

Melissa's moist blue eyes were wide and disingenuous, and held quite honest outrage, but that careless definition hurt.

"I don't think you assessed his possible reactions very well," Lou said, feeling rather shocked. "Men, I imagine, can do as crazy things as women on the spur of the moment if they've been made fools of."

"Yes, that was it, of course," Melissa said, sounding complacent, then her eyes narrowed.

"If you know that much, Lou, you should have known better than to steal him," she said with hard deliberation, "for that's what you did, didn't you?"

"I don't think so. It was you who threw him over, after all."

"And you had such little pride that you snapped up my leavings before he could change his mind. Shy, unsophisticated Miss Mouse – how we've all underrated you."

Lou turned away and, to control her own not easily aroused temper, busied herself with drawing the curtains across the windows. The cottage lights still winked in the darkness, but the water was black and empty of any craft and the wind was rising.

"You aren't making it very easy for me to make you welcome here, Melissa," she said then, and her cousin came quickly across the room and put a conciliatory hand on her shoulder.

"Sorry, darling," she said. "I was just being bitchy. My nerves are all shot to pieces. You – you won't let Piers turn me out, will you?"

"You heard him say you can stop till tomorrow."

"But you'll persuade him to a little longer, won't you – just to get my bearings again?"

"I don't understand why you came here in the first place. Had you any ideas of getting Piers back?"

"Now who's being bitchy? I told you, Blanche turned me out."

"Why? Cousin Blanche got what she wanted from Piers. She made it very plain to me that so long as she wasn't dunned for the money she couldn't care less which bride he chose."

Melissa moved away and sank into a chair, drooping elegantly.

"Darling, how hard you sound – not a bit like little Lou Parsons," she said plaintively. "Has Piers succeeded so quickly in changing you?"

"Piers and you and Cousin Blanche have all changed me, perhaps," Lou replied soberly. "I'm not, you see, little Lou Parsons any more."

Melissa bit her lip, unsure, for the first time, of the right reply. With marriage, the little cousin of no importance seemed to have grown another skin.

"And is the honeymoon coming up to expectations?" she asked, prompted by genuine curiosity, but Lou's newly acquired armour was not yet proof against careless probings. Melissa saw her flinch before she replied briefly: "Naturally," and her charming mouth curved in a slow, satisfied smile, but she made no comment except to ask to see her room.

"I don't know where Tibby will have put you," Lou said, aware that it could not be long before Melissa would see for herself how low she rated in Tibby's eyes.

"Is that the old scarecrow who let me in?" Melissa asked, following her cousin across the hall and up the stairs, observing with shuddering distaste the ascetic bareness of Piers' home.

"She used to be Piers' nanny – a rather difficult old lady, so go carefully," Lou answered.

"Oh, yes, I've heard Blanche mention her. I believe she was rather devoted to my mama. We should get on nicely," Melissa said complacently, and Lou had no doubt they would, if for no other reason than that Tibby would enjoy making unflattering comparisons. Oh well, she thought, it was only till tomorrow; she could afford to allow Melissa her accustomed homage until then.

They opened bedroom doors, hunting for a room which had been prepared for the guest, and Melissa, uninvited, looked into Lou's room.

"This must be it," she said. "I will say it looks a bit more civilised than the rest of this morgue-like house."

"No, this is my room," Lou said, and felt herself colouring as her cousin's eyes dwelt pointedly on the single bed.

"My poor Lou!" Melissa said with laughter bubbling up through the tones of commiseration. "No wonder you shied away from my innocent cracks about the honeymoon. How long is it now – two weeks, three?"

"Piers sleeps in there," Lou said stiffly, jerking her head towards the dressing-room. "It's – it's quite usual these days to have separate rooms."

"Oh, quite – but hardly on a honeymoon," Melissa poked her head round the door of the adjoining room, discovered that the beds were a pair and enquired with amusement:

"Who had the bed moved in there – you or Piers?"

"That," said Lou, the knowledge sweeping over her that the day's delicate approach to the night must, perforce, be already doomed to sterility, "is a rather impertinent question, don't you think? We'd better find your own room."

The room was, it transpired, directly across the passage from hers and she wondered if Tibby had deliberately chosen it. A fire had been lighted, and Melissa's cases unpacked, and the bowl of flowers Lou had so painstakingly arranged for Tibby's pleasure had been brought up from the kitchen. The rejected offering hurt her unreasonably. Tibby could have taken any one of the many flower arrangements which filled all the rooms. It would seem to be a quite deliberate snub on her part.

"What a lot of luggage you brought," Lou said, surveying

the several suitcases piled in a corner. "It was hardly worth unpacking everything for one night."

"It might be for longer if Piers is handled tactfully," Melissa said, and Lou turned on her cousin, her patience snapping at last.

"Really, Melissa! Even you wouldn't force yourself on a couple wanting privacy at a time like this," she exclaimed, but Melissa only smiled that slow, impervious smile that could be proof against any insult.

"I should have thought in the circumstances you might have found it a relief. It can't be much fun living in splendid isolation on a dreary island with a tardy lover," she said with a slight drawl, and Lou experienced a most unusual desire to slap her cousin hard across her charming face.

"That was unforgivable," she said. "I'm going down now to see that Piers makes arrangements in good time for the launch to take you across to the mainland in the morning. You'd better start packing again tonight."

But when morning came Piers said it was too rough to cross with any comfort. The wind had risen alarmingly during the night, but Lou knew instinctively that the weather was not, as yet, too bad to deter him had he wished to make the trip. She had no means of guessing what had transpired after she had gone up to bed last night – for Melissa had deliberately out-sat her hostess – and Piers, morose and silent for most of the evening, had made no move to second her suggestion that their guest might like to go to her room. Lou had left them by the dying fire and it had seemed a long time before she heard Piers moving about next door. She had known that her dream of the day's ending was lost to her, but he did not even look in for the customary goodnight, and long after the line of lamplight under the dividing door had been doused to darkness she lay, tossing uneasily, listening to the wind and the sound of the breakers, praying that the storm would hold off long enough to allow the passage of a launch to the mainland in the morning.

Piers took himself off soon after breakfast and would be all day, Tibby said, dealing with the business of the island, checking stores, sharing his midday meal with the islanders to save time.

"Best stay indoors, missis, 'tes getting rough," Tibby said, and Lou asked quickly and without due thought:

"But not too rough for the launch?"

Tibby smiled.

"Not if Mr. Piers had a mind to chance it. Been across to the mainland in worse weather than this, but like as not he's no taste for the trip."

"What do you mean?"

"What I say, missis. The young lady makes pleasant company, and after all, she was his rightful bride, wasn't she?"

Lou made no reply, used by now to the old woman's strange delight in causing embarrassment, but she wondered unhappily what, indeed, had made Piers change his mind overnight. Melissa, when at last she put in an appearance downstairs, gave no hint, neither could Lou ask her, but the older girl had about her the settled air of a guest on an indefinite visit, and for that day at least showed a visitor's polite deference to the wishes of her hostess. They spent the hours of daylight chatting inconsequently over a roaring fire, and Lou, relaxing against her will, realized that this must be the first occasion when she and her cousin had shared such lengths of intimacy together. It was, she realized, however, no guide to her cousin's make-up. Melissa was merely being smart and amusing at her friends' expense; the slick little clichés, the brittle catchwords, were all part of a familiar gambit designed to impress, and Lou wondered why Melissa should have thought her worth the effort. Her cousin's incessant chatter to the accompaniment of the transistor set she had brought with her began to have no meaning, and Lou, feeling drained, longed for Piers' return, knowing at the same time that once he was with them, Melissa's interest would be immediately switched.

He came back to the house when darkness fell, and Lou sensed at once that his mood of yesterday had changed. He was once again the Piers Merrick she first remembered; the raffish, rather world-weary young plutocrat whose slightly waspish humour did not match the warmth of his voice, and who seemed to slip back so easily into the familiar superficial interchanges with Melissa.

"You're very silent, Cinderella," he said, his attention suddenly focussing on Lou, making her jump. He was, had she known it, very much aware of that stillness in her which had first attracted him; of the way the lamplight fell on her smooth hair and long neck, of the touching look of a dressed-up child one of those unsuitable trousseau dresses gave her, and his mouth tightened, remembering Melissa's innuendoes of the night before. He wanted no unwilling bride who was ready to confide her fears and doubts to the first inquisitive listener.

"Well?" he said impatiently, "haven't you anything to contribute to the conversation?"

"I haven't had much chance of joining in," she retorted mildly, then unwisely added: "If the weather doesn't worsen you'll be able to make the trip to the mainland with Melissa tomorrow, won't you?"

Piers made no comment, but his smile was not pleasant, and Melissa sent him a little sidelong glance of amusement.

"My truthful Cousin Louise couldn't be plainer, could she?" she said with a small pout. "Speed the parting guest and all that. Still, Lou darling, I do sympathise. I *have* gatecrashed the honeymoon, after all, and that should be a social blunder – or shouldn't it?"

"It depends on the honeymoon, I imagine," Piers said carelessly, and this time there was no doubting the edge to his voice and the smouldering spark of anger in his eyes.

"Of course. I didn't mean to be rude, Melissa," Lou said quietly, but she bit her lip as she saw her cousin's expression of smugness and the little look of complicity she threw to Piers. Whatever devious methods had been employed last night, Melissa had done her work well or, more likely, Piers, faced unexpectedly with the fruits of his own folly, had realized too late where his affections lay.

"I wouldn't blame you, darling, if you *were* rude, but the situation has its piquancy, hasn't it?" Melissa said, and Lou knew that she was enjoying herself. She was not sure that in a cynical, inverted sort of fashion Piers, too, might not be capable of deriving amusement, if not pleasure, from this embarrassing affair, and she sprang to her feet, suddenly unable to bear this ill-assorted triangle any longer.

"I'm going to wash my hair," she said, because it was the first excuse that came into her head, and having made the statement, felt bound to comply with it.

As she soaped and rinsed her tears mingled with the water and she found herself sobbing without control because this way only was there relief from the trap in which she found herself. How dared Melissa pry and hint and patronise? How dared Piers side, at any rate by implication, against his wife? But of course she was not his wife, she thought wearily. Tibby knew, and Melissa knew, and whatever construction they chose to put on the situation, the shame was hers, not Piers'.

She sat on the floor drying her hair by the fire in her room, drawing comfort from the small familiar chore. There was still an hour or more before dinner would be ready, time to gather fresh courage while the two downstairs exchanged their unknown confidences, even indulged, perhaps, in mutual regrets. She remembered, then, Piers saying on their wedding night: "I never regret things. If they don't work out I just forget them or throw them away . . ." Had he decided so soon to cast her off, to make handsome reparation for his mistake, no doubt, but to adjust to the foibles of the rich with no great inconvenience to himself?

Lost in her own unhappy speculations, she did not hear him come upstairs, but suddenly she was aware of him standing in the doorway between their two rooms. He was looking down at her with faint surprise, as if he had not expected to find her there.

"So you really did mean to wash your hair?" he said.

"But I said so."

"I imagined it was a feminine excuse to get out of the room. You shouldn't let Melissa get away with things so easily, you know."

"And what," asked Lou with a spurt of anger, "do you suppose she's trying to get away with? You could have taken her to the mainland this morning if you'd had a mind to."

"So I could," he said, advancing into the room to stand over her. "I understood, however, that it was you who had begged her to remain – to ease an awkward situation, one must suppose."

"Melissa said that?"

"Oh, I don't blame you, Lou. You could hardly be expected yet to learn to dissemble for the sake of your pride, but it's a pity you gave yourself away so completely."

"How do you mean?"

"You know very well. I would have thought you'd have had more nous than to blurt out the dreary details of the failure of our honeymoon, and to Melissa of all people."

"I've discussed nothing of our personal relations with Melissa," she replied, indignation lending her courage. "She's simply drawn her own conclusions from what she's observed — and, I suppose, what she must instinctively know."

"And what's that?"

She turned her face away, bending her head to the warmth of the fire, shaking the remaining drops of water from her hair.

"That she should have been in my place. That we both made a great mistake, that — "

"So you think we made a mistake?" His voice sounded remote and impersonal above her head.

"Well, don't you think so?" she replied, surprised to find her voice quite cool and steady. "You implied a moment ago that I hadn't enough pride, Piers, but I think it's your own pride that's been hurt. You don't like Melissa to know how easily she could get you back, do you?"

"What the hell are you two cooking up between you?" he demanded furiously. "I listened to her last night out of consideration for you, since you had made me out an ogre, and I hoped to find out why, but if you don't want her here then I'll send her packing tomorrow, but for God's sake make up your mind."

He squatted suddenly on his heels beside her and turned her round from the fire to face him, and as he became aware of her defenceless expression, his hard features began to soften. There was a nursery air about her, he thought, as she sat curled up on the floor in a dressing gown, the soft fringe damp and childish on her forehead, and the unmistakable traces of recent tears on her flushed cheeks.

"You've been crying," he accused. "For heaven's sake, what am I doing to you, my poor Cinderella?"

She leant towards him, the tears ready to overflow again at the kindness back in his voice. Could she make him understand, even now, when she understood so little herself?

"Everything's spoilt — " she said. "I thought — I'd hoped — "

"What did you hope for? The happy-ever-after ending to the fairy tale?"

"That's what you promised, didn't you?"

"Did I? Rash in the circumstances, perhaps, but one can always carry on with the makebelieve."

"Was it only that for you? Is it Melissa who's real, after all?"

"Melissa is no more real than I am, perhaps," he replied enigmatically. "That's why I – well, at the time we seemed complementary. Can't you understand?"

"In a way. But things are different now, Piers, surely? Won't you send her back tomorrow?"

She thought he hesitated too long before giving his reply, and when he did speak he sounded ambiguous and not too encouraging.

"You realize, I suppose, the stories she'll spread around? After your girlish confidences, you no less than I will be a laughing stock."

"Isn't that why you married me in the first place – to avoid being made a laughing stock?" she asked gently. She was too tired to deny again that she had confided in her cousin, and judging by his small twisted smile he would not have believed her if she had. Melissa would scarcely have had to embroider very much to convince him of his own shortcomings as a lover.

"I am, it would seem, a rather irresponsible person when it comes to something as serious as marriage," he said, getting to his feet. "If it's what you really want, however, we'll send Melissa home tomorrow. Far from turning her out, I've no doubt Blanche sent her here in the first place, so you don't need to have a conscience."

"Cousin Blanche? But why should she – "

"Oh, be your age, Lou!" He was tired and disturbed and her ingenuousness suddenly irritated him. "If the marriage had gone through as planned your insatiable cousin as mother-in-law to a rich man would have had an endless pull on my purse-strings, but as a mere cousin by marriage many times removed, she scarcely qualifies for further charity, does she? Hadn't you better be getting dressed? Dinner will be ready in half an hour, and I imagine you'll want to match our guest's warpaint with some of your own. I'll go down and break it to the lady that she'd better start packing."

But Melissa, of course, did not go. All that evening she behaved beautifully, having apparently accepted gracefully Piers' ultimatum of an early departure. She was, Lou thought, rather over-dressed for a quiet evening at home, but the effect was highly satisfactory. She struck delightful poses, made amusing comments, charmed an unwilling host back into ease, and deferred politely to Lou as became a guest. This time she was the first to retire gracefully to bed, embracing her cousin affectionately and blowing a discreet kiss to Piers.

"Thank goodness for that," Lou said, drawing a deep breath. "I thought there might have been a scene."

"You don't know your cousin very well, do you," Piers retorted. "Melissa only makes scenes as a last resort."

"Does she? Well, there was hardly anything to make a scene about, was there?" Lou said, feeling a shade uneasy. Piers' eyes at times resting on Melissa's lovely, discontented face had, if cynical, still been admiring, she thought, with the same unconscious look of appraisement she had seen him give to any pretty woman. He would, however, be scarcely human, she supposed, if he did not remember that only a very short while ago he and Melissa had made love together and planned marriage.

"I mean," Lou blundered on a little helplessly, "it wasn't reasonable to come in the first place, was it? She could hardly expect – "

"She would probably argue that my change of brides

wasn't reasonable either, so what?" Piers retorted dryly, and she lowered her lashes, not wishing to meet that suggestion of mockery in his eyes.

"Then," she said, because despite the knowledge that it was unwise to argue with him on such a delicate subject she liked logical conclusions, "she shouldn't have quarrelled with you and run off with someone else in a pet."

He laughed in spite of himself and pulled her out of her chair.

"Very true, Miss Prim. Now run off to bed while I deal with some letters I want to post on the mainland tomorrow. We'll make an early start if the weather will let us," he said.

But it was not the weather which delayed Melissa's departure. The wind and the sudden squalls of rain had lessened considerably by morning, and Lou, waking to find Tibby standing by her bed with the customary early tea-tray, felt a great relief as the curtains were drawn and a watery sun gave promise of a better day.

"She'll not be leaving yet," Tibby said, immediately quenching the relief. "Been sick all night, she says, poor maid."

Lou's hand shook as she poured the tea. Her unease of the night before returned in force as she remembered Melissa's exemplary behaviour, the suspicious lack of argument or please for extended hospitality.

"It's a trick!" she cried, uncaring that the old servant's smile was sly and pitying at the same time. "I heard nothing in the night."

"Maybe you slept too sound. Mr. Piers was up."

"Piers? But surely he would have called me?"

"Maybe yes, maybe not. Who's to say that they mightn't have wanted to be alone?"

"If you're trying to make mischief, Tibby, you're going the wrong way about it," Lou said coldly, and Tibby shrugged and shuffled to the door.

"The mischief was made when Mr. Piers brought you

here instead of that other one. Go see for yourself if you don't believe me," she said, and left the room.

Lou jumped out of bed and seizing a dressing gown, hurried across the passage to Melissa's room. Whether Piers had been disturbed or not seemed of little consequence then; it was easy enough, she thought, to fool a man with imaginary illness; she had not, herself, been above providing vague symptoms to satisfy an obliging doctor in her school-days.

Melissa greeted her wanly from a bed which bore evidence of frequent tossing and unrest. Lou, prepared for an act she had every intention of exposing, had to admit that her cousin looked ill. Her face had a waxen tinge which was not induced by any cunning use of make-up and her forehead was damp with little beads of sweat.

"Sorry, darling," she mumured. "It doesn't look as if I'll be a starter for the homeward trip today."

"What's the matter with you?"

"Don't know — must be something I ate. That old woman brought me some foul potion to settle my stomach, but it only made me sick."

"Tibby? Had you gone to her?"

"No, she came to me — said she guessed I wasn't feeling well. I felt a darn sight worse after she'd dosed me. She woke Piers, too."

Lou gave a little shiver. It was, of course, ridiculous to imagine that Tibby could have had any part in Melissa's indisposition, but on the other hand she was plainly gratified that the departure must be postponed, and surely it was odd to rouse the master of the house in the case of illness and not the mistress?

"How do you feel now?" she asked, trying to put some concern into her voice, and Melissa gave her a faint, mocking grin.

"Lousy," she replied. "Apologies and all that, darling, but with the best will in the world I couldn't face a heaving ocean today."

It was very clear that she could not, and when she closed her eyes and rolled over on to her side with the weary lack of interest of someone who only wanted to be left alone, Lou went away. She met Piers in the passage, fully dressed, carrying a tray bearing a small array of medicine bottles and a glass.

"Oughtn't we to get a doctor?" she said, and his smile was amused.

"Hardly worth sending over to the mainland for a bilious attack," he replied. "This little lot should settle a queasy stomach rather better than Tibby's home-brewed muck."

"Why didn't you call me in the night?" she asked, and his eyebrows lifted.

"Why disturb you when there was nothing you could do? Tibby was there."

"Tibby seemed to know without being told that Melissa wasn't feeling well, and her patent remedy appeared to be the finishing touch," Lou said with point, and saw Piers frown.

"I don't know what you're trying to imply by that, but I'd advise you not to let your imagination run away with you," he replied with distinct coldness and, brushing past her, knocked on Melissa's door and, once inside the room, closed the door firmly in his wife's face.

The day passed uneasily for Lou. Although Melissa remained in bed and made few demands on anyone's time, she could not rid herself of a feeling of foreboding.

By tea-time Melissa was sufficiently recovered to have made up her face and chosen a becoming bedjacket in which to receive visitors. Lou, who had been keeping an anxious eye on the weather all day, suggested that her cousin should make the effort, if possible, to travel tomorrow before the threatened storm could break, and was discomfited when Melissa turned with a grin to Piers and said:

"You should be flattered, darling, by your come-by-chance bride's anxiety to be alone with you. How do you still work the old charm on this godforsaken island with no tempting distractions to offer?"

Piers, quite unembarrassed, replied with a flippant rejoinder, but later, when they were alone, Lou said with unfamiliar bitterness:

"Come-by-chance . . . that's what I am, aren't I?"

"Your grammar is questionable and your supposition faulty," he replied, but his regard was kindly. "You should know your cousin well enough not to take her seriously."

"But she only spoke the truth. It's what everyone must be saying."

"Then we must prove everyone wrong, Cinderella. After tomorrow, we'll begin again."

"Do you think she'll be well enough to travel?"

"I don't see why not. A slight tummy upset is hardly a lingering complaint."

Lou, reassured, was grateful to him for a brief return of the Piers she had been beginning to know, and even Tibby, appearing with her familiar unexpected suddenness to observe in passing that such matters were decided for us by those above, failed to dampen her hopes. But it was Tibby who, an hour or so later, came downstairs to inform them that Melissa had been very sick again and would certainly not be fit to leave in the morning.

"She was all right at tea-time," Piers said sharply. "Have you been dosing her with your unspeakable concoctions again?"

He did not wait for a reply but went upstairs to see for himself how bad Melissa might be, but Lou, watching the old servant's retreating back as she went to the kitchen, was certain in her own mind now that Tibby's potions were the main cause of the trouble. For her own reasons she wanted Melissa to stay, and, thought Lou, it was by no means beyond the bounds of possibility that her home-brewed remedies could contain some harmless irritant that would cause vomiting.

She said as much to Piers when he came downstairs again, but he was no longer receptive.

"Nonsense!" he exclaimed crossly. "You'll be suggesting next that the poor old girl cooks up poison in her spare time."

"Not poison – just something harmless to cause sickness," Lou said, and a small note of distraction came into her voice. "Can't you *see*, Piers? Tibby's done her best to drive a wedge between us ever since you brought me here. She must know perfectly well that our marriage isn't – isn't normal, and she's taken a fancy to Melissa. She wants to get me out and Melissa in."

She stopped speaking abruptly as she felt the sudden chill in Piers' regard.

"You're talking a great deal of rubbish," he said coldly. "The speculations of a rather ignorant old servant should hardly concern you, and whatever Tibby thinks you have largely yourself to blame. You give so much away."

"How can I help it when you made it so clear at the beginning – separate rooms and – and everything? It was you who gave too much away, not me."

"At least I didn't confide your apprehensions to Melissa."

"What do you mean?"

"You know very well, my dear. You begged her to remain in the first place as a possible distraction, and now you're stuck with her you have second thoughts."

"You know that's not true! If Melissa told you I had confided in her she did it for her own ends, and one needn't look very far for them."

"Indeed?"

"Yes, *indeed*! You called her bluff, you see, by marrying me instead of chasing after her, and now she has regrets."

"Possibly we all have regrets," he said, sounding suddenly

very angry, "but whatever yours may happen to be, don't imagine that you can use your decorative cousin as a red herring. We'll see if you're so pleased to be rid of a convenient excuse when I send her home tomorrow."

"Oh, Piers, we're quarrelling . . ." Lou said inadequately, valiantly resisting a sudden desire to cry. She could not know that to give way to tears just then might have broken down his resistance, for she had none of Melissa's instinctive knowledge of the right and the wrong moment for exercising feminine wiles, so she merely sounded petulant and childish.

"Hardly a quarrel," he replied crushingly. "The whole thing's a storm in a teacup and not worth any loss of temper. You're carrying your makebelieve a little far, Cinderella, when it comes to turning Tibby and Melissa into a witch and the wicked fairy respectively. You must learn to grow up."

"One can't," said Lou, listening to an ominous rise in the wind which could mean that the storm would break before morning, "grow up, if one's treated as a child. You have, I think, a very limited experience of women, Piers."

He looked at her with surprise, hearing, too, with slight uneasiness, the change in the weather. She could be right at that in her assessment, he thought a little ruefully, remembering the brief, sophisticated affairs which had punctuated his life. There had been scant, reality in any of them, and there was something very real, and a shade disturbing, about this child he had married so inconsequently. Had Melissa not arrived to interrupt his tardy wooing, he might, by now, have found that simple felicity which had always eluded him, and which he had instinctively felt could be fostered on this island cut off from the tedious obligations of wealth.

"You're probably right," he said. "It's even possible that you can teach me more than I can teach you. Forget my impatience, Lou, if you will. Tibby's potions, whether they were responsible or not, shall be poured down the drain in future, and we'll have Melissa headed on her homeward journey tomorrow. Will that satisfy you?"

CHAPTER SEVEN

But the storm broke in the night. Lou had lain listening to the violence and fury of wind and rain and known that her last chance was lost. Inexperienced in matters of west country weather, she had thought the last couple of days wild enough, but, looking from her window in the morning at the heaving sea, and the giant waves turning the little harbour into a cauldron, she knew that departure from the island now would be impossible.

"How long will it last?" she asked Tibby.

"Days – could be weeks," the old woman answered, but there was, oddly enough, no triumph in her voice, only indifference. Having got what she wanted, Lou realized, she could afford to withdraw her spite, or perhaps she was merely sitting back and waiting.

Melissa, Lou found, had recovered sufficiently to leave her bed and devote time and care to her face. Tibby had unpacked again for her, and when Lou looked in to enquire, she was making a leisurely and dissatisfied selection from the mass of clothes she had brought.

"Not a rag to wear! You've got away with the best of my wardrobe, darling," she said, flinging yet another rejected garment in a heap on the floor.

"You can take back anything you want," Lou said flatly. "I've worn hardly any of them."

"Can I really? Even the mink?" Melissa's disgruntled expression changed promptly to one of charming excitement. "Let's go and make selections at once, shall we?"

She ran across the passage to Lou's bedroom without waiting to be asked, and Lou stood watching while her cousin pulled her clothes from their hangers, trying them on, tearing them off, admiring herself from every angle.

"After all, they were meant for me, weren't they?" she said, finally wrapping herself in the mink coat with sensuous delight, preening complacently over the rich fur held against her throat, fully aware that such a coat could do for her what it never would for Lou.

Neither of the cousins were conscious of Piers until he spoke from the doorway of the dressing-room.

"What the hell's going on?" he demanded. "This room looks a shambles."

"I'm only taking back some of my possessions," Melissa said, posing deliberately for him to admire and approve.

"*Your* possessions?"

"Well, they were bought for me, darling. Lou has very sweetly said I can have them back."

"As I understand I'm responsible for the bills, the decision hardly rests with Lou," Piers said, and there was a dangerous softness in his voice which would have warned Lou but was lost on her cousin.

"Well, even so, sweetie-pie, you'd hardly grudge me some of the spoils, would you? Look at all I've lost by flirting with temptation, which is all it really was. Besides, Lou isn't the type for sophisticated glamour and you can well afford to buy her a demure little trousseau of her own. After all, what girl wants to take on another girl's leavings?" Melissa had probably spoken at random, and was referring to the clothes, but Lou caught her breath, and Piers heard.

"So you've been complaining again, complaining and confiding?" he said to her, quite pleasantly, but his expression was not pleasant as he watched the betraying colour creep under her skin.

"Melissa, you know I never mentioned – " Lou began, but Melissa's fine blue eyes had narrowed and her slow smile was politely apologetic.

"Well, darling, perhaps you sometimes *are* a little naïve with your confidences, but *I* understand, of course," she said. "Piers, you mustn't expect too much of your little bride. Our Louise is devastatingly truthful, you see. If she feels disappointed or – or – cheated, she makes no bones about it."

"And do you feel cheated, Cinderella?" The mocking bite was back in Piers' voice and he flung the nickname at her with none of the accustomed gentle humour.

"I don't think our private affairs can have much interest for Melissa," said Lou, striving for dignity, but before he could comment Melissa broke in with drawling amusement:

"On the contrary, my sweet. You forgot that Piers and I were once engaged, and anything affecting his love life interests me profoundly. Darling Piers, can't I even keep the minky?"

"No," said Piers harshly, aware with a distaste in himself that when she chose to cajole him with her old practised guile, she could still stir his senses, if not his reason.

"Oh, let her have it," Lou said wearily. "I'm not all that way about mink, anyhow."

"Shut up, the pair of you!" Piers exclaimed rudely, and went back to his dressing-room, slamming the door behind him.

"Poor sweet! Between us we've really got him rattled," Melissa remarked, her head on one side, and Lou, driven at last beyond the polite bounds of hospitality, rounded on her cousin.

"Melissa, we'd better come to an understanding," she said. "I'm stuck with you, thanks to Tibby's efforts and this blasted weather, but if you came here to make mischief you'd better have second thoughts, so no more hints and half-truths about confidences I've never made. Leave Piers alone – understand?"

It never failed to surprise Melissa when her mousy little cousin suddenly turned. She had not learned, as Piers was beginning to, that under that artlessness lay a simple honesty that could be disconcerting.

"Why, darling – " she began in injured protest, then her curiosity got the better of her. "What do you mean by Tibby's efforts?"

"Those doses she made you swallow. They had something in them to make you sick, hadn't they? I believe you knew it, too."

For a moment Melissa looked surprised, then she laughed.

"Really, Lou, I begin to think Piers is right when he says you live in a world of makebelieve and are no flesh and blood wife."

"Did Piers say that?" Even as she spoke, Lou despised herself for asking the question, and Melissa seized her advantage. Lou might be hard to fool over certain things, but on the subject of Piers she was vulnerable.

"That was the kindest of his criticisms," she retorted. "You really shouldn't have jumped into marriage with a man of his type and expect to hold him at arms' length. Can I keep the mink, darling?"

Lou had gone a little white, but she managed to speak calmly.

"If Piers agrees. He's paying for it."

"Oh, he'll agree if you talk him round nicely."

"All right, we'll make a bargain," Lou said, suddenly shedding the first of her too sensitive skins. "You want that coat badly, don't you? If you behave yourself while you're here you shall have it, if not, you won't."

Melissa hugged the coat around her and gazed reproachfully over the soft, rich collar.

"Honestly, darling, I don't know what you're getting at," she protested, and Lou turned away and began putting clothes back on their hangers, conscious that her hands were trembling.

"I think you do," she said. "Now help me tidy up the room, please, and first I'll have the coat back."

Melissa took it off reluctantly, then flung it on the floor with sullen petulance.

"It sounds suspiciously like blackmail to me," she said, and Lou unexpectedly grinned.

"What's a little blackmail between cousins?" she replied with airy unconcern, aware, to her own amazement, that it was surprisingly easy to call her cousin's bluff, once you knew how.

But it was not so easy, Lou discovered, to maintain that advantage when Piers was present. Melissa gave a good enough impersonation of the untimely guest who had unwittingly outstayed her welcome to make him frown at Lou's lack of response.

"You're hardly helping the situation," he told her. "Melissa's sudden arrival was unfortunate, if altogether typical, but at least she's behaving herself. Why can't you play ball?"

Because, thought Lou wretchedly, you could never win playing ball with Melissa, but she could hardly tell him so.

"I'm afraid I don't know the rules," she temporised, and he gave her a sharp look.

"I only meant make an effort to be more natural – more of a hostess," he replied mildly. "There's only the one accepted rule for polite hospitality, surely?"

"Do you think I'm being rude, then?" she asked, sounding anxious and bewildered again, and he made a small gesture of impatience.

"Good grief! How literal can you get?" he exclaimed. "Of course you're not rude – it's only – oh, well, if you don't get my meaning, I can't explain. Forget it."

She got his meaning all right, she thought, but doubted whether he himself was as clear. He was being made to feel ill at ease by the situation, and whatever he had felt for Melissa during their engagement could surely not, Lou thought, be forgotten so soon.

She tried, after that, to be more social and attentive

141

when the three of them were together, but it was not easy to forget that she had once been the Chaileys' poor relation, expected to be grateful for the crumbs, and Melissa, although she was too clever to openly disregard her cousin's new status, had subtle ways of reminding her that make-believe was no foundation for security.

"Cinderella!" she would say with a giggle. "Is that Piers' charming nickname for you?" Lou had ceased to find it charming and she knew Melissa knew it, too. "But darling, what could be more romantic? The press fairly went to town on the story – or don't you read the gossip columns?"

"We don't get the papers here – at least – "

"Of course you do! They come over by launch with the mail; Tibby's kept the lot. Really, Lou, you have no sense of occasion – or does Piers keep the sordid details from his Cinderella bride?"

"What was sordid about it?" Lou asked with innocent surprise, and flushed as she realized how ingenuous she must sound.

"That was a figure of speech, you clot!" her cousin retorted, starting her familiar aimless perambulations round the room. "You really will have to take a pull on yourself, sweetie, if you're not to bore Piers to death. As a novelty for a jaded appetite he may find you refreshing, but he's got to spend the rest of his life with you – or has he?"

"And what do you mean by that?"

"Well, these days marriage isn't the ghastly till-death-do-us-part affair it used to be. Divorce has become respectable – and *very* fashionable."

Lou controlled herself with an effort. She knew that she laid herself open to ridicule by her ignorance of the easy standards of the rich which made her say stupid things, but at least she could deny her cousin the satisfaction of getting a rise every time, so she held her tongue and merely blinked back.

Two days went by with the storm still raging, and it became difficult to fill the long hours between meals. Piers was out of doors a great deal, helping the islanders with their livestock, and the makeshift repairs to their homes, but the two cousins had to make do with each other's company and the small transistor set Melissa had brought with her. Lou missed her daily rambles on the island and her shy exchanges with the fishermen and their wives. She would have welcomed an opportunity of helping Tibby about the house had she been wanted, but the old servant did not mellow with their enforced captivity and refused all Lou's tentative offers. It was all the more galling, therefore, to find Melissa perched on the kitchen table at odd moments, drinking tea and smoking her Turkish cigarettes, while Tibby ironed or baked, apparently unresentful of interruption.

Lou found herself becoming gauche and awkward, knowing that that was how Melissa wished to her to appear, and sometimes she caught Piers looking at her with with impatience, even with irritability. She had no weapons with which to match Melissa at her own game, for she had never learnt the art of verbal hide-and-seek. Piers, she reflected, for all his professed experience of women probably did not realize how subtly she was being stripped of confidence, or how often his eyes rested on Melissa with speculation and, it could be, regret.

She was aware that now she retorted sharply and often with childish petulance when he teased her, so that he began treating her with an exaggerated politeness in Melissa's presence which was more hurtful than his casual banter; also she was afraid. This inopportune visit was no whim, she had begun to realize, neither was the blame laid on Cousin Blanche probably true. Melissa had unintentionally burnt her boats by running away for a kick, as she had expressed it, but now she wanted Piers back, and even if she could not have him for herself, she could very well wreck Lou's marriage.

On the third evening after she had slipped away early to bed, apparently unnoticed by the other two, Lou lay awake, listening to the storm and waiting with increasing trepidation for Piers to come up. She must, she thought, have the courage to get certain things clear between them, but when, at a very late hour, he answered her call and stood in the doorway between their rooms, she could not remember what they were. He made no move to come into the room and had the air of a polite stranger willing to perform a trivial service but anxious not to be detained.

"What did you want?" he asked.

She could think of nothing but the proverbial childish excuse.

"A glass of water, please."

"It's by your bed."

"Oh – oh, yes, of course. Piers – "

"Well?"

She struggled up against her pillows, aware that she dealt clumsily with slipping bedclothes, that one of Melissa's elaborate nightgowns appeared on her ridiculous rather than inviting, and such questions as she would have liked to ask could only sound impertinent.

"Well?" he said again, and this time she forced herself to remember that she was his wife.

"I want to know how long this is going to last," she said, and his eyebrows shot up with unamused tolerance.

"My dear child, I don't control the weather," he replied, and she said with brave doggedness:

"I didn't mean the weather."

At once she was conscious that he stiffened, that during those hours when she had so foolishly left him alone with Melissa he had suffered a sea-change. He did not, it became clear, even intend to afford her the solace of the usual tucking-up routine and blessings for the night.

"Piers – " she said, drawing up her knees under the bed-clothes and clasping her arms tightly around them, "I – I don't think you quite understand my position. It – it isn't very nice to be a cypher in one's own home."

"You don't," he retorted quite pleasantly, "make much effort to assert yourself, do you – except to stress a shrinking for your husband's possible advances?"

"Is that what Melissa told you?"

"Melissa gives a good deal away unintentionally. She doesn't understand maidenly modesty. She has a very healthy attitude towards sex."

Lou's indecisiveness vanished in a sudden surge of anger.

"Very obviously," she snapped. "You or this other man – healthy, possibly, but hardly discriminating – or doesn't that matter?"

For a moment he looked taken aback, and even a little scandalised, as if a child had unwittingly thrown a dirty word at him.

"What are you trying to imply?" he asked coldly, and she put her head down on her knees, answering from the muffled folds of the eiderdown with the forlorn defiance of a child that knows it is beaten by adult logic but refuses to give in.

"Only what you yourself are implying – that you and Melissa realize your mistake – that I'm just the stumbling block. You once told me that if things didn't work out you just forgot them or threw them away. You — you want your freedom, I suppose."

The silence that followed was so long that she thought he must have gone away. She was crying now, dismayed by her own lack of reticence and the evil genius which had made her blurt out such unconsidered opinions when she should have taken a leaf out of her cousin's book and played it cool.

"Does that mean you want yours?" he asked then, and his voice seemed to come from a long way off. When she made no reply he appeared to hesitate, then she heard him move and when he next spoke he was standing by the bed looking down at her.

"Poor Cinderella ..." he said with gentle regret. "I've given you a raw deal, haven't I? Melissa's made me see that very clearly ... she says, quite rightly, that you aren't the sort of girl to play games with."

She looked up then. The wind which, despite the well-fitting windows, had found out the cracks, made the lamp flare in a sudden gust, causing shadows to flicker across his face, giving him a strange expression.

"Was it only a game?" she asked, aware that too late a ghost of the old tenderness was back, that had she pleaded with him, or simply confessed her own doubts and misgivings, he might have at least offered her comfort.

"No," he answered. "A thumbing of the nose, perhaps, even a rather ill-considered gesture of defiance, but never a game. Don't cry, Cinderella ... I'll put things right for you. Just pretend in your makebelieve for a little while longer. When you come back to reality again this will all seem like the dream it is."

"And isn't the island *your* makebelieve?" she asked, tightening her hands round her knees. "Don't you, when you come to Rune, escape from reality and enjoy a fairy tale of your own?"

He stood there, looking down at her, the expression on his lean dark face suddenly unsure.

"Clever of you," he murmured softly. "Yes, perhaps we share the same need, after all, my dear ... Go to sleep, now."

She automatically lifted her face, but he did not kiss her. The hour was so late and the ceaseless noise of the storm so hypnotic that she could no longer think clearly — if, indeed, she ever had.

"Goodnight," she replied, and lay down obediently, making no further effort to detain him. He turned down the lamp, pinching out the wick with practised fingers, and went back to his own room.

Lou awoke to an impression that the storm had abated. The sea seemed to break with less savagery against the rocks, and today it might be possible to get out of doors. If she could escape from the confines of these four walls for a time she might be able to sort out her unhappy problems or at least reach a compromise with herself. It had not occurred to her as yet to fight for her happiness, for had not Piers, on his own showing, confessed to a realization of his mistake, and in admitting his folly would lose no time to rectify it?

She slipped out of the house before Melissa was down, and for a moment staggered against the porch as she met the force of the wind. But she had learnt the island's geography by now and knew where the sheltered places lay. The rough scrub which was Rune's principal vegetation had been torn up and scattered in wanton profusion and some of the cottage windows were crudely boarded up where the glass had been blown out, but along the shore, in the lee of the cliffs, there was sufficient shelter to make walking possible and it was good to smell again the salt and the seaweed and feel the sting of wind and spray.

Forget it or throw it away . . . forget it or throw it away . . . the waves seemed to beat out monotonously, and a curious change came over Lou. Last night's sad acceptance of the end of her fairy tale began to give way to a sense of outrage. She was Piers' wife in law, whatever the circumstances, and the law was on her side. Until she was convinced in actual fact that it was Melissa Piers wanted, she was not going to help him to jump out of marriage as quickly as he had jumped into it.

Brave resolve, she thought, turning homewards, or only wishful thinking? But her old doubts returned as she entered the house again and experienced the familiar sensation of trespass. Piers and Melissa were chatting companionably over pre-luncheon drinks, and Lou might have imagined that they paused long enough in their interrupted conversation to make her feel she was intruding. She did not, however, imagine the sudden constraint in Piers' manner, reminding her that last night's bitter interchange between them was still unresolved.

Becoming conscious of both her cousin's possessive ease and her impeccable grooming, Lou was tempted to turn tail and do something about her own dishevelment, but instead she demanded a drink. Piers looked surprised, for she seldom drank spirits, but he poured her a gin and tonic without comment except to suggest with unnecessary point that it might be better if she went upstairs to tidy.

"Presently, when I've had my drink – possibly two drinks," he replied calmly, and Melissa giggled.

"Darling, you are breaking out!" she said. "Piers is right, though – you can't image what a little scarecrow you look in those dirty old slacks, with your hair standing on end."

"Personally, I think she looks rather charming," Piers observed unexpectedly. "No one dresses up on Rune."

Lou was grateful for the polite snub, but Melissa pouted.

"Is that meant for me?" she asked plaintively. "You used to be both observant and critical of your girl-friends' appearances, Piers. Why, only just now you were saying that poor Lou – "

"I'm not aware that we were discussing Lou," Piers interrupted on a cool, warning note, and Melissa lowered her long lashes and smiled up at him through them. She did not contradict him, but Lou thought there was a world of meaning in the look, and the smile, and, ungratefully, she now felt angry with Piers for his defence of her. They had quite obviously been discussing her, and it was the first time she had known Piers to be a little embarrassed.

"Well — mud in your eye, and here's to holy wedlock!" she said with sudden defiance, gulping down her drink and holding out the glass for more.

"And what do you suppose you mean by that? I think you're a teeny weeny bit tiddly already," Melissa said, but Lou thought Piers gave a faint grin. He refilled the glass and returned it to her gravely, advising her to drink more slowly.

"You should get out of doors, Melissa," Lou said with her new-found composure. "It's not too rough today to walk, and tomorrow it might even be safe for the launch to put out, mightn't it, Piers?"

He made no reply, observing her thoughtfully, but Melissa, recognising a new, unsuspected quality in her cousin, said quickly:

"Dear Lou, you sound in a most unflattering hurry to get rid of me. Have you been consulting the oracle?"

"The oracle?"

"The voice in this phoney cave Tibby's always talking about. It's supposed to warn you of impending doom or something."

"You didn't go to the cave, did you?" Piers asked sharply, and Lou looked bemused, her small advantage already lost.

"No," she replied. "What did you mean, Melissa? Piers says the cave legend is just superstition."

"Of course it is, but Tibby believes," Melissa said carelessly. "Was it really a temple, Piers?"

"Very probably — though whether the Druids had anything to do with it is a moot point. I've told you, Lou, to keep away." Piers spoke so curtly that both girls looked at him with surprise.

"I haven't been there since that first time," Lou assured him, and Melissa said, with a small gurgle of laughter:

"I think you must believe in it too, Piers. Well, well, imagine the hard-boiled, worldly-wise Piers Merrick succumbing to local superstition! That *will* be a laugh when we all get back to civilization."

"If it amuses you to jeer, you're welcome," he retorted. "The cave has a bad name, that's all. A girl drowned there."

"But you said the cave never filled except in time of storm," Lou began, her eyes wide and startled at this unexpected evidence that her own feelings about the cave had not been misplaced, and Tibby, entering the room with her usual soft-footed secrecy to announce that lunch was ready, chipped in as if she had been part of the conversation.

"And it's a time of storm now, missis," she said. "It was a time of storm when that other maid died – too afraid to live with her own conscience, so they say."

"Why? What had she done?" Lou asked, repelled yet fascinated by the gaunt old woman's Cassandra-like utterances.

"She had stolen another woman's mate," Tibby replied, with a long, piercing stare at Lou, and Piers rose angrily from his chair, knocking over his glass with a careless gesture of annoyance.

"Keep your bedtime stories for anyone silly enough to listen, Tibby," he snapped. "If one were to believe all the grisly legends that Cornwall boasts we'd be drowning in pools or jumping off cliffs from sheer suggestion. Take that dazed look off your face, Lou, and go and get tidy."

Piers went out immediately after lunch, and Melissa, once the need to appear gay and amusing had been removed, poured out an incessant flow of grumbles and ill temper. She needed a hair-do, she was sick of fish and those endless stodgy soups and puddings, the battery of her transistor set was nearly finished and without it life could not be endured, and she was out of cigarettes. No one would believe, she concluded waspishly, that the gilded Piers Merrick enjoyed playing at the simple life in such discomfort.

"Rune isn't a game. It's real for Piers," Lou said, but her cousin made a rude noise.

"Don't kid yourself. He's only a little boy playing king-of-the-castle," she retorted. "But enough's as good as a feast, as you will find out. *I* would soon have talked him out of that caper."

"Would you, Melissa? But you tried, didn't you? That was the quarrel that proved your undoing."

"It proved something else, too – that my quiet, mousy little cousin wasn't above rushing in for the kill."

Lou was sewing a button on one of Piers' shirts, aware that this wifely chore annoyed her cousin unduly, but she was irritated herself now, and bit off a thread with a sharp little snap of teeth which told Melissa she had scored a hit.

"Well, you did, didn't you? Very clever, darling – all that lovely lolly just for the taking."

"You should know by now that Cousin Blanche scarcely has patience with girlish scruples, and the lovely lolly was important to her."

"You're saying she pushed you into it – so what? Blanche was scared. If she hadn't lost her head she'd have tried to find me, or at least given me the red light."

"Since you stated in your note that love was the only thing that counted, she might be forgiven for not understanding that you were only out for kicks," Lou said crisply. "Besides, Piers wouldn't wait. If I hadn't agreed he'd have found someone else."

"So what have you gained, Cinderella? Not very nice, surely, to be picked at random, and you're hardly the type to hold a man's who's married you out of pique. You can see for yourself he's come back to me already."

"Don't call me that," Lou said sharply, then she laid down her work. The morning's walk had sharpened her wits if it had not entirely cleared her thoughts; now was as good as any time to have things out with her cousin.

"I don't know what you mean to imply by that, Melissa, and I don't want to know," she said, "but I think it's time we understood each other. You're trying to take Piers away from me, aren't you?"

Melissa shrugged. If she was surprised that mousy Cousin Lou was prepared to do battle she was quite unperturbed. It might be amusing to see how far the silly little thing would go to fight for her imagined rights.

"You can't take away something that's never been possessed," she retorted a little cruelly, and had satisfaction in knowing from Lou's sudden wince that that remark had struck home.

"First blood to me," she observed mockingly.

For a moment Lou's innate honesty nearly defeated her intentions. It was only too true that there was no physical bond between herself and Piers, and last night he had all but admitted his mistake. *Pretend in your makebelieve a little longer*, he had said, and that, surely, could have meant only one thing.

"You're in no position to know what's been between us since we married. Men can make do with substitutes better than women can," she said with a gallant attempt at pretence, but Melissa simply laughed derisively.

"Tell that to the marines, darling!" she scoffed. "I've seen your virginal couch, don't forget, and in any case one can always tell. Besides, Piers confides – and more than that, he takes what he wants where he can get it. Too bad, my sweet – but you have grounds for divorce if you want."

For the second time since Melissa had come to the island Lou wanted to slap her, and this time she did. She slid forward quickly to the edge of her chair and without further thought caught her cousin smartly across the cheek with the flat of her hand.

For a moment Melissa said nothing, but her blue eyes held an ugly expression. Temper had drained the colour from her face and the red mark of the blow stood out angrily on her cheek.

"You'll be sorry for that," she said then in a soft, deliberate voice. "You'll be very, very sorry, you little bitch — you little thief!"

She left the room before Lou could stammer out an apology, and presently she could be heard talking in high tones to Tibby in the kitchen. She was enlisting Tibby's sympathy, Lou supposed, just as, later, she would certainly enlist Piers'.

Lou sat on disconsolately, aware that all the headway she might have made, the reasoned things she had meant to say, were defeated by that ill-considered slap. She observed with sadness that Piers' flowers, which she had arranged in such loving expectation only a few days ago, were already dying, and all at once she felt too tired to fight any longer. There was no sense in clinging to what you had never possessed, and if Melissa was what Piers wanted then let him have her. It had, after all, just been makebelieve, an impossible dream; the sort of dream any little wide-eyed bridesmaid might have while envying the lucky bride. It was time and more to wake up.

She apologised to Melissa the next morning, but meeting her cousin's contemptuous expression, was reminded of Piers' advice. *Never apologise to anyone who shakes your self-confidence,* he had said . . . *the world takes one at face value* . . . And Piers' world was, of course, Melissa's. Only last night when he had looked into her room to wish her the customary courtesy of pleasant dreams, he had added impatiently:

"Why do you have to upset Melissa?"

So taken aback had Lou been that she had stammered some incoherent reply that only made him frown.

"Why is it two women can never get on together?" he had exclaimed, and Lou's temper, not improved by an evening listening to her cousin charming her husband, and being tolerant to herself as though nothing had happened, flared up again in ill-considered speech.

"That's a very masculine and idiotic statement," she retorted. "There's no particular sex distinction in not getting on with somebody else. What's Melissa been telling you?"

"Nothing that you'd be very pleased to hear, I imagine."

"Very likely! She suggested a few things to me, as well, that I didn't much care to hear."

"Such as?"

"That you took what you wanted where you could get it. The implication was obvious."

His face froze so suddenly into a mask of icy distaste that she shrank back against her pillows, and when he next spoke it was with the voice of a complete stranger.

"If you're expecting a denial of that sort of statement, Lou, you'll be disappointed," he said with deceptive mildness. "You clearly have so little opinion of my morals that we'd best leave it at that."

"I," faltered Lou, suddenly drained of argument, "haven't asked for a denial. I – I have to accept the fact that you just made use of me – that Melissa's unlucky intervention put paid to what chances I may have had."

She had surely, she thought much later, given him some indication that her own desires had importance, that even then she would have humbled her pride had he spoken one kind word, but his expression did not change, and when he did reply she heard such anger and such bitterness in his voice that she had no words left.

"You talk like an ill-used servant, and underpaid at that," he told her with cutting sarcasm. "If you can believe that I'm the kind of man who will make love to another woman with my wife sharing the same roof, then you're certainly entitled to that freedom you spoke of the other evening, for you and I clearly have nothing on which to build a relationship. Goodnight."

He had, thought Lou when he had gone, finally slammed

the door in her face. She should have known him better, she supposed, than to allow the day's mischief to come between them, yet what knowledge had she of this reputedly raffish stranger she had married than the little he chose to let her see.

So in the morning she apologised to Melissa partly as an act of penance, partly because her own good manners regretted the slap, and she said as much.

"I told you you'd be sorry, didn't I?" her cousin said. "And I didn't just mean the shamefaced amends of a child."

"I'm not shamefaced except for my temper," Lou said gravely. "And I think you'll agree I had provocation, but let's forget it."

"You may forget it, darling. *I* won't. You look washed out. Had words with Piers again? He took himself off early this morning to potter round his blasted island."

"He lends the fishermen a hand. The storm's doing plenty of damage."

"I suppose so. Too rough for a boat, still, would you say? I'm right out of cigarettes now, and the radio battery's quite dead."

"You can get cigarettes from the store."

"But not Turkish, and I'm sure the store doesn't sell the right sort of batteries. Sam Smale would go to the mainland for me."

Melissa's petulant voice became soft and coaxing on the last sentence, and Lou gave an exclamation of exasperation.

"Really, Melissa, you're being utterly unreasonable!" she said. "Do you imagine Piers would allow one of his men to risk his life in this storm just to satisfy a selfish whim?"

"Piers needn't know," Melissa said, with a pout. "Besides, the storm seems to be abating, and Tibby says the launch has crossed to the mainland in rougher water than this."

Lou's patience snapped.

"If it's possible for the launch to go out, then it's possible for you to go with it," she replied sharply, and saw the faint look of surprise her cousin gave her.

"I couldn't weather this, darling, I should be sea-sick," she said reproachfully. "Oh, well, I'll have to do without my small necessities, I suppose, though how I'm going to fill the time without my radio, I can't conceive."

"You can read an improving book, or go for a walk," Lou retorted, and Melissa stretched slowly, admiring with satisfaction the sleek, supple lines of her own body.

"I might at that – go for a walk," she replied unexpectedly. "Do you feel like showing me that Druid's Cave?"

"No," said Lou shortly. "I haven't been there again."

"Scared of hearing the spook voice?"

"There's no voice, it's an echo."

"Well, perhaps you're just scared of the legend coming true. You've stolen another man's mate, to quote Tibby, haven't you, darling?"

Lou sighed. It was becoming very hard, she found, to ignore Melissa's pricks and goads by trying to remember that she was still the hostess.

"I'm not a child, Melissa, to be frightened into a state of guilt by threats of bogies," she said, and Melissa laughed.

"I didn't suppose you were. As to a sense of guilt – well, I was just being bitchy. I'd probably have done the same myself if I'd been in your place." Melissa spoke with such an unexpected change of heart that Lou looked at her suspiciously.

"You've been doing your best to break things up since you've been here," she said slowly, and her cousin made a wry little face.

"So I have," she agreed with charming frankness. "I couldn't resist giving you a few uncomfortable moments because I felt sore. It looks as if I shall have to settle for that mink, after all, doesn't it?"

Lou had forgotten the mink and her own feeble attempts at blackmail. This, she thought with relief, was perhaps Melissa's way of calling a truce, of admitting herself beaten. It would not be easy, perhaps possible, to wipe out the mischief so deliberately sown, but it was not in Lou's nature to be ungenerous.

"You shall have the mink, of course, and anything else you want of what was, after all, your own trousseau," she said. "In return, just tell me one thing. You were lying, weren't you, when you implied that you and Piers – ?"

"Just fabricating, darling, which is different, knowing you'd run off to accuse him. You did, didn't you?"

"Yes, I did, and I've hurt him mortally."

"What a grandiose phrase! Didn't he deny it?"

"Not in so many words, but Piers wouldn't, would he?"

Melissa shrugged and gave a tiny yawn.

"I wouldn't know," she said indifferently. "All I've ever learnt from life is not to ask gentlemen awkward questions. Be warned, Cinderella, or the glass coach may turn back into a pumpkin."

It was so much the kind of remark that Piers himself was wont to make if he wanted to evade an issue that for a moment Lou was startled.

"Do you really want me to show you the cave?" she asked awkwardly, with the naïve artlessness of a child offering to share a secret as a sop, and Melissa frowned impatiently.

"Of course not. I don't believe Tibby's half-baked yarns, and you shouldn't, either. Why don't you make one last visit yourself to cock snooks at the spooks? Spit in the sacred pool, or something, to lay the curse. Go on – I dare you!" Her impatience had given way to an air of charming devilry. So, in other days, had she exhorted her more timid young cousin to stick up for her rights.

"No," said Lou. "I don't like the place. It's evil."

"Be your age, Lou! How can a damp old cave be anything more than cold and slimy? I'll tell you what – go this afternoon and I'll buttonhole Piers and try to put him right on a few vexed questions. I owe you that much, anyway. All right?"

Lou was tempted. Who, she thought, but Melissa herself could undo the harm that had been done?

"Well ... she began doubtfully. "No. Piers said keep away."

"Only because he's jealous of his find, like a small boy. He discovered the cave, didn't he? He doesn't like sharing his island or anything on it, but you'd soon cure him of that if you're clever. Look – when I've confessed my sins to him I'll tell him where you are so that he can go quickly off for the grand reconciliation scene. He'll fall for that one – Blanche always said he was a romantic at heart."

"No," Lou said again, but with less firmness, and Melissa blew her a kiss and changed the subject.

Lou had not intended to fall in with her cousin's highly fanciful scheme for the simple reason that life had already taught her that things rarely worked out as one planned. By the time luncheon was over, however, she felt a need to escape into the open. Piers, eating his meal in a morose silence which even Melissa seemed unable to break, added little to the civil demands of hospitality. Tibby, waiting on them with unusual abstraction, appeared for the first time to be showing her age, muttering to herself, forgetting table appointments, and failing to react to Melissa's little jokes.

Lou went, with a sense of release, into the open air and the buffeting wind which, though knocking the breath out of her to start with, seemed to blow away the confusing issues of the past twenty-four hours.

She scrambled over rocks, and splashed through pools, making for the comparative shelter of the part of the shore that was flanked by the cliffs. The tide was coming in, she saw, breakers sending up a curling wall of foam and spray, but the sands still stretched, uncovered with water, to the cliffs. Great heaps of seaweed, torn from the rocks, blew wildly across the shining expanse, and gulls swooped sharply, scavenging for food, their screams harsh and shrill on the wind.

Without realizing it Lou had come upon the fissure in the rock face which led to the Druid's Cave, or perhaps, she thought uncertainly, fingering the smooth, cold stone, a visit to the cave had been at the back of her mind, despite her denials to Melissa. For all her first antipathy to the place, she had been piqued by Piers' refusal to take her back, thinking him churlish to resent his discovery with her. For all the sinister tales Tibby had attributed to it, the cave had still been beautiful and strange, and Lou thought, only her own imagined danger of drowning had given her that sense of evil in the first place. Just once more, if it were only to test her own rational common sense, would she venture, and be able to say on her return that she had accepted her cousin's childish dare and could agree that there was nothing to cause discomfort but damp and cold, and wet feet.

She squeezed through the narrow aperture, and as she felt her way along the passage, the sudden quiet was uncanny. The sound of the storm evidently could not penetrate to the heart of the cliffs; just every so often a whistling whine echoed down some unseen cranny in the rock, dying away to leave only the monotonous dripping of moisture down the walls.

Lou traversed the passage with more assurance this time, knowing that there were no pitfalls, apart from the broken ground, before she came to the cave itself. Despite her intention to revisit the place, treating it simply as a curiosity, however, she began to experience the tremors of that first fear. She was relieved when the passage began to widen, telling herself that she had merely been suffering from a very common form of claustrophobia, but when she emerged from the gloom, with the same sense of shock as before at that sharp spear of light cutting across the darkness of the cave, she felt no easier.

It was all just as she remembered it, the rough altar, the pool, the myriad reflections of light from the stalactites, the half-seen outlines of the crude carvings. She stood as she had then, in a shallow pool of water, staring and wondering and little awed. The cold was intense, the clammy, moribund chill of a place which had never seen the sunlight, and with a little shiver, Lou turned to go. Honour, if that had been in question, was satisfied; she could escape now, and she would not come again without Piers.

Sounds of the storm outside had filled the cave with no more than a ghostly whisper of eddying moans and sighs seeping through the high aperture which let in the light, but as she moved carefully towards the mouth of the passage, a new sound joined them. At first it was only a low wail, rising and falling as might the wind, then it took shape, echoing eerily from the rock face, the vaulted roof, the very stones beneath her feet, stopping her in her tracks.

Lou ... ou ... ou ...! it seemed to say, and Lou turned back to face the cave, her lips stiff with sudden fear.

"No !" she shouted frantically, and heard the echo of her own voice flung back to her, *Oh ... oh ... oh ...!*

CHAPTER EIGHT

SHE laughed then, the sharp, staccato laugh that relieved tension, and that, too, came back to her as an echo. How idiotic can one get? she thought; the wind had merely been obliging with its traditional whoo-oo-oo, but even as she chided herself, the sound came again, this time in the shape of words which could hardly be misinterpreted.

Lou . . . ou . . . ou. . . Give back . . . ack . . . ack what you've stolen . . . another man's mate . . . ate . . . ate . . .

"It's a trick!" cried Lou, and the last word echoed back to her with the same hollow sadness of that other voice, and then left silence. The silence was almost more frightening than the voice, and as she waited, the sound of her own heart beating was loud in her ears. She turned once more to go, trying to control her rising panic, and the voice spoke again, disembodied, sexless in its echoing overtones.

Go away . . . way . . . way . . . it wailed. *He doesn't love you . . . he doesn't want you . . . Give back . . . ack . . . ack before it's too late . . . ate . . .*

"Who are you?" shouted Lou. "I don't believe in ghosts — well, not really."

I am the Voice . . . I am the voice of the drowned to warn you . . . ou . . . ou . . . Lou . . . ou . . . go away . . . he doesn't want you . . . Rune doesn't want you . . . you're just a come-by-chance . . . ance . . . go away . . . way . . .

Reason deserted Lou. All Tibby's tales and warnings came back to choke her with terror and she began stumbling round the cave in a last desperate attempt to trip the trickster in whom she no longer believed, but there was no one there. The altar stone concealed nothing but slime and grotesque fossils which might once have been living creatures, the walls had no hidden recesses and the pool was black and evil-looking, but unruffled. She sank down on the wet stones, beginning to grasp the frightening, uncontrollable sobs of panic, waiting like a trapped animal for the voice to speak again and, like an animal, afraid to move. But the voice did not speak, and after a long time she summoned up enough courage to shout a challenge.

"Are you there? Have you finished?" she called, but only her own voice came back to her.

She was by now so incapable of coherent thought that she imagined that if she moved the voice would return to stop her, that somewhere an eye must be observing her, that if she remained very still and perhaps prayed, the evil presence would go.

It was a fresh sound, however, that finally roused her to action, the sound of water slapping against rock, the swift little advances and withdrawals of a steadily moving stream which had not been there before. Lou became aware that the stone floor of the cave on which she had been sitting for so long was no longer slimy but otherwise dry. Water was lapping over her ankles and knees, and she got hurriedly to her feet, only to sink down again with a cry of agony as cramp attacked her legs. As she sat there frantically trying to massage back the circulation she looked towards the passage opening, and saw, with a totally different kind of fear, that water was pouring through. She remembered Piers telling her, with a certain degree of scorn for her early fears, that the cave never filled, except in times of storm. But this was a time of storm, and the tide had been coming in. Was she then to drown like that poor girl of the legend? Was this the manner in which she must give back what she had stolen?

"But I've stolen nothing!" she shouted, returning suddenly to sanity by reason of a more tangible terror. "And I'm hanged if I'm going to climb on to that beastly altar stone and wait meekly for death ... I'll drown fighting if I have to drown at all!"

There was no one to hear the foolish bravado of her shouted defiance, but the sound of her own voice helped to restore her nerve. She struggled once more to her feet, ignoring the aches and pains that still shot through her legs, and splashed clumsily towards the passage and began to fight her way out. Sometimes the water was only around her ankles, sometimes well above her knees as she stumbled over the rough, uneven ground. Often she fell, wrenching her ankle so badly at one point that she thought she would be unable to go any further.

She remembered that Melissa had promised to send Piers to find her if she went to the cave, and remembered, too, that she had told herself, with more sense than she now appeared to possess, that most likely she would wait in vain for a deliverer who never came. It was all the more astonishing, in the circumstances, to hear his voice shouting above the wind as she at last reached the entrance to the passage and the blessed daylight, and saw Piers' tall figure splashing through the boiling surf, now up to the foot of the cliffs. He must have passed the entrance to the cave without a second thought, for he was walking away from her.

"Piers!" she screamed after him. "Oh, Piers, come back!"

He turned at once and came back at a run, his oilskins flapping, his hair wild in the wind and his dark face a curious mixture of alarm and anger.

"Good God! You haven't been in the cave, have you?" he demanded, catching her by the shoulders with hands that shook a little.

"Why didn't you come in to find me?" she asked, aware suddenly how narrowly he had missed finding her at all. "Melissa s-said she'd send you."

"What the hell's Melissa got to do with it? I haven't seen her since lunch," he replied roughly, and shook her until her teeth chattered. "You senseless bloody-minded little idiot! Don't you realize that in another quarter of an hour or so you wouldn't have got out at all? Why should you suppose I should think of looking for you in there?"

"Because of Melissa," she repeated stupidly, and burst into tears. "Piers – I heard the voice," she sobbed incoherently. "It said I was to give back what I'd stolen – I was to go away – you didn't want me – Rune didn't want me. It was the voice of that poor drowned girl . . ."

The roughness went out of his hands and his voice alike and he held her against him, smoothing her wet head with gentle reassuring fingers.

"All right, Lou, it's all over now . . . you've had a bad dream, but it's all right now. Come along home," he said, and she clung to him tightly.

"You don't believe me, do you? You think I'm making it up, but there *is* a voice – Tibby's right."

"I believe *you* believe it, darling, but that's another story. You're all in, aren't you?" he replied, and she gave a little sigh.

"You've never called me darling before," she said, able to be astonished even in the midst of her distress, then remembered last night and the monstrous accusation she had thrown at him which had hurt him so bitterly.

"Piers," she said, "I shouldn't have said what I did last night – I shouldn't have believed Melissa."

"No, you shouldn't," he replied a shade grimly. "Still, I'm beginning to think I've been a bit bedevilled myself. I too should have known better than to listen to your cousin's fairy tales."

"Fairy tales are for children – grown-ups shouldn't believe them. I don't believe in mine."

"You're all mixed up, my poor dear, and it's no wonder. Whatever you thought you heard in that infernal cave has shaken you up, hasn't it? What on earth made you go there?"

"To make my peace, perhaps – to bargain with the gods or whoever they are in there. But if Melissa didn't tell you, why were you looking for me, then?"

"Because you'd been out a long time and tides are tricky in times of storm. I thought at first you'd been crazy enough to go with the launch."

"The launch?"

"Didn't you know? Your irresponsible cousin persuaded Sam to go to the mainland for cigarettes and a radio battery. I ask you – risking life for a radio battery!"

"Piers, no! Was it safe? Will he be all right?"

"Oh, Sam's a good enough seaman, though he's no right to use the launch without permission, and if it's damaged I'll have the hide off that selfish little bitch. I'll have the hide off her anyway after this. Did she know you were going to the cave?"

"She suggested it. You don't think – you *couldn't* think she meant me to *drown*!"

"No, I don't think that, but I'm beginning to have certain rather unpleasant ideas about your voice. Perhaps you didn't imagine it, after all. Come on, my dear, if we stay much longer we'll get caught by the tide."

He had to help her, for her twisted ankle was too painful to stand much more walking, and presently he picked her up and carried her, slung across his shoulder like a sack. She was too exhausted to try to work out for herself the implication in his last remarks; she only knew she was safe, that his uncomplimentary references to Melissa hadn't sounded much like those of a man in love, and that he had addressed her as darling as if he had meant it.

By the time he had reached the house she was half asleep, and after that things seemed to happen with bewildering unexpectedness. Piers gave curt orders, and Tibby, unfamiliar in role of comforter, hastened to obey. Lou barely recognised her old enemy in the woman who, with painfully working face and trembling hands, ministered to her needs like the nanny of her imagination.

"Don't worry, Tibby," Lou said shyly, while she submitted to a harsh and vigorous towelling after a bath which had been almost too hot to bear. "Piers says Sam is an excellent seaman, and it's not far to the mainland, is it?"

" 'Tes the vanity of it – the sinful vanity, putting a soul in peril for a passing fancy," Tibby said, and her lapse into the island idiom was proof of her disturbance. "Sam should have known better, 'tes true enough, taking the boat and all, but she flattered him with her serpent's tongue, dared him, for sure, to risk his life for trash."

"My cousin's spoilt," Lou said, feeling in duty bound to make excuses for Melissa, and Tibby snapped back, with a last, ungentle flick of the towel:

"Aye, like her mother before her. Miss Blanche had the same pretty ways, the same disregard for others."

"But you loved her, didn't you, Tibby?"

"Loved? No, we was more like mazed, all of us – young Mr. Robert Merrick as he was then – Piers because she smelt nice and promised the first woman's love he had know, and I because I was past my first youth even then and never man nor maid had looked at me twice."

Lou stood in humble stillness, unconscious of her nakedness or Tibby's hard gaze slowly softening as it rested on her young, pliant limbs. Three people, caught up in a dream, she thought, just as she herself was caught now.

"Is everything just makebelieve?" she asked, and the old woman smiled, the difficult, unwilling smile of someone unused to capitulation.

"Life is what you make it," she replied. "And dreams don't last. Mr. Piers maybe knew what he was doing, after all, when he picked you for his bride. Pleasure him, missis – don't be affeared of all that lordly act he puts on. He's always liked to play big."

Lou would have liked to embrace Tibby, but felt it was too early yet to take liberties which might be misunderstood. She reached instead for her dressing gown, and turning too quickly on her injured ankle, was reminded by the sudden pain of her ordeal in the Druid's Cave.

"Tibby – " she said, knowing that here, at last, was someone who would believe her story, "I heard the voice. Piers thought I was dreaming or imagining, but I heard it distinctly. It warned me, just as you said – the voice of that drowned girl."

Tibby's reaction was unexpected. No sly triumph at the vindication of her prophesies came into her face, only a puzzled doubt.

"Of what did it warn you?" she asked.

"To go away – to give back what I'd stolen – another man's mate, it said – your very words."

"H'm ... m ... now that's a strange coincidence. Did it say Piers loved another?"

"Yes, it did. Tibby, how do you know these things? It wasn't – it wasn't you playing tricks on me, was it?"

"No, it wasn't me, missis," Tibby replied a shade grimly, "though my words were used."

"You mean there is no voice?"

"Oh, aye, according to legend. Some believe and some don't, and it was a long time ago."

"Even so, you tried to scare me, didn't you?" Lou said accusingly. "You wanted to drive me away. You wanted my cousin in my place." Even as she spoke it seemed strange that she could accuse her enemy so brashly.

"Because she was his rightful bride, and because I saw Miss Blanche in her ... 'tes lonely here on Rune ... strange thoughts come in the dark nights ... and ghosts. I had thought with Piers marrying Miss Blanche's daughter to slip back down the years, you see, and then he brought you here and it was as if I'd been tricked."

"I see," Lou said gently, wondering for a moment if Piers had not been right when he had remarked so casually that his old nurse was getting senile, then suddenly she understood. Tibby was only another victim of makebelieve. Living alone for months at a time, perhaps, on this island, she had woven her own fantasies out of the past, because all her life reality had only come to her through others.

She stretched out a hand to touch the woman's face with tentative solicitude, surprised to feel the moisture of tears.

"If you'd accept me now, Tibby," she said shyly, "we can still make the dreams come real – some of them. You – you would like nurseries again, wouldn't you?"

Even as she spoke Lou felt herself flushing scarlet. What right had she to think of nurseries when her husband held her at a distance and Tibby herself had schemed and prevaricated over the marital bed from the beginning?

Tibby observed the blush with a sardonic eye, thinking no doubt, Lou reflected with embarrassment that Piers' come-by-chance bride was getting inflated ideas of her prospects, then that unfamiliar, reluctant smile began to twitch at the corners of the woman's thin lips.

"Happen you'll suit at that," she said, and someone hammered loudly on the bathroom door.

"What in Hades are you two up to?" Piers' voice demanded irritably. "You've been in there long enough in all conscience. Lou, you should be in bed, and I want to bandage that ankle. Can I come in?"

He opened the door without waiting for permission, observed his wife's heightened colour and a look on Tibby's face that he had not seen since his nursery days, and grinned.

"The lamb lying down with the lion, I observe," he said. "Tibby, you old faggot, it's about time, too, you had a change of heart!"

"You'll need a change of heart yourself, Mr. Piers, before you start calling me names to my face," Tibby retorted, but his grin only grew wider.

"Haven't I always called you names to your face?" he replied, then his mood altered abruptly. "Sam should have been back by now. I'm a bit worried."

"What's the time?" Lou asked anxiously.

"Gone six. I've a good mind to take the second launch and make a recce."

She looked at him with eyes widened in alarm.

"But that's crazy!" she exclaimed. "What's the sense of risking two boats – two lives, perhaps? Sam may have got held up on the mainland with the weather – or anything. Piers – "

He took her hands, holding them with kindly reassurance but also with firmness.

"I'll give him another half-hour," he said, "but after that you mustn't try to keep me. I have a responsibility to my islanders, you see. Understand?"

"Yes," she said, remembering Melissa's taunts about king-of-the-castle games. But this was no game, and Rune no toy to satisfy a rich dilettante's whim. This unpredictable stranger, she knew now, was the real Piers Merrick, and at last she understood what he had meant when he had told her that in bringing her to his island he was paying her a compliment.

Lou stubbornly refused to go to bed. Her hot bath and Piers' dose of brandy would have warded off a chill, she said, and she refused to be packed off upstairs until there was news of Sam. She did not add that if Piers fulfilled his intention of making a search himself, she could not endure the hours of waiting lying inactive in her bed, but he probably guessed, for he gave in without argument, and his smile was tender as he tucked her up on a sofa by the fire in the living-room.

"Where's Melissa?" she asked, discovering with surprise that this was the first moment she had missed her cousin.

"Keeping out of my way, I imagine. I've had no time, as yet, to deal with that young woman," he replied a trifle grimly, and she glanced up at him through her lashes. It was, she thought, very gratifying to hear that irritable note in his voice directed, for a change, at her glamorous cousin.

"You must be fair to Melissa," she said, however, striving for fairness herself. "She wouldn't have had any idea of the danger when she talked Sam round. She's so used, you see, to young men fetching and carrying for her."

His expression, she thought, was suddenly rather odd, and when he replied, the old impatience was back in his voice.

"You really do ask for it, don't you, Cinderella?" he said, and made her feel foolish at once. "Here you are, defending a girl who has no loyalty to you, and expect me to be fair to her. What did you mean, incidentally, when you said Melissa would send me to the cave?"

"We'd planned it – at least she had, only at the last minute I said I wouldn't. She – she was going to – "

"Going to what?"

But Lou could not go on. He had told her that he had not seen her cousin since luncheon, so it was clearly impossible that Melissa had straightened out the tangle. She and Piers, thought Lou, remembering now with embarrassment the things she had said to Tibby, were no nearer a tacit understanding than they had been. She had, she supposed, read too much into his concern for her. It was only the same responsible concern which he felt for Sam.

"Tell me, Lou, this voice you heard – was it female?" he asked, and she gave him a puzzled frown, wondering why he should return to a subject he had dismissed as imagination. The warmth and the sense of security, the pleasant aftermath of her frightening experience in the cave had almost persuaded her that she had dreamed the whole thing.

"I couldn't tell," she replied sleepily. "It was a disembodied voice – like the weird sound effects one sometimes hears on radio. Did I dream it, after all, Piers?"

"Not to worry," he said, looking down at her with a quizzical twitch of one eyebrow. "You've never quite woken from your original dream, have you?"

"Oh yes, I have," she said, suddenly wide awake. "You must get out of the habit, Piers, of thinking of me as Cinderella. There comes a time when fairy tales outlive their uses."

"So they do," he replied, with a little grimace of surprise and affection. "Well, stay awake, Lou – I may have need of your clearer vision. I must go down to the harbour now – time's getting short. Take a nap till I'm back."

When he had gone, however, the desire for sleep went with him. If he came back with no news of Sam and the launch, he would, she knew, set out himself. She had no knowledge of what danger that might involve, but she knew that until he was safely home again she would have no peace of mind.

The force of the wind had lessened, she thought, listening to the now familiar buffetings of the storm. It would, she reflected, beginning to grow sleepy again, be quite strange to have silence once more and the recognisable, intermittent sounds of the island which were no more than a passing assurance of life. She was nearly asleep when the sharp click of an opening and shutting door roused her and she saw that Melissa had slipped into the room.

"Well!" her cousin observed, moving into the circle of lamplight, "you've certainly got what you wanted at last! Piers in a tizzy – even the scatty old girl running round in circles. You should thank your fairy godmother, Cinderella."

"Why?"

"For turning the pumpkin back into a coach, of course. The cave idea was a good one, wasn't it?"

"No," said Lou, "it wasn't. I might have drowned."

"Really, darling, that's a little much. Didn't your reluctant bridegroom come to the rescue, just as I said?"

"Yes, but you didn't send him as you promised. You never meant to put things right for me, did you?"

"More pressing matters came up. I was out of cigarettes and a radio battery, but never mind, Lou ... ou ... ou ..."

Melissa had turned away as she spoke and her last word could have been distorted by coinciding with a sudden gust of wind, but Lou, realizing with a sense of shock what Piers had probably already guessed, knew her cousin well enough to appreciate that Melissa could not resist a reminder of her own cleverness.

"*You* were the voice!" she exclaimed, and for a moment, relief that there had, after all, been nothing supernatural about her ordeal in the cave made her curious rather than angry.

"I was rather good, don't you think? I might even have succeeding in driving you away if you hadn't run into Piers. That was my bad luck," Melissa said, and a sense of outrage rose in Lou.

"What a cruel thing to do – what a mean, despicable trick!" she cried. "You'd no intention of talking to Piers – had you? You'd no intention of sending him to look for me. Did you know the cave filled in times of storm? Did you want me to drown?"

Melissa flung herself into a chair, stretching her arms above her head in one of her deliberate poses of grace.

"Of course not," she said impatiently. "And anyway you didn't, so why the drama? It's paid off very nicely for you as things have turned out, hasn't it?"

"Why did you do it? You'd made enough trouble for me without that, surely," Lou said, trying even then to find excuses for a prank which could have ended disastrously.

"I did it for kicks," Melissa replied, adding with a shrewish bite: "And I did it for the pay-off. I said you'd be sorry for that slap, didn't I? Sam Smale showed me how."

"Sam!"

"Oh, he wasn't involved in any plot, poor lamb, he just knew the trick of the echo; all the islanders know it, apparently. There's a certain spot where you stand outside and speak down a funnel in the rock. I couldn't see you, of course, Lou, but I bet you panicked more than somewhat. What a pity it was all wasted. I – " Melissa broke off so abruptly that Lou's horrified attention became diverted. She followed the direction of her cousin's hastily turned head and saw Piers standing in the doorway.

"Go on," he said, "what else had you planned to make a Roman holiday?"

For the first time Melissa's assurance deserted her. She wriggled forward nervously in her chair, forgetting her former elegant pose, and tried to bluster things out.

"Darling, don't make a thing of it," she said. "I only played a harmless trick – just for kicks. No one's a penny the worse."

"No? You seem a little too fond of playing for kicks. Wasn't that your excuse for running out on me?" He spoke so mildly that she was misled into brashness.

"Yes, it was, and you should have known it instead of making a fool of my simple little cousin just to get your own back," she said, flinging a contemptuous glance at Lou, and Piers took two long strides across the room and stood over her with hands clenched at his sides.

"Get out!" he said. "Get out of here before I administer the sort of kicks you haven't bargained for. You've never wanted me, Melissa – only the satisfaction of making a successful kill. Even that was playing for kicks, wasn't it? When you'd gone one better than the Joneses you'd have been looking round for something else to relieve the boredom. Get out!"

"Even you," said Melissa, her voice a little unsteady, "can hardly put me out into the storm – or can you? Lou – "

"I," said Lou with total unexpectedness, "couldn't care

less. I've been pushed around long enough – now it's your turn."

Despite his anger, Piers gave a faint grin, but Melissa looked at her cousin as if she saw her for the first time.

"Lou, you wouldn't . . . you couldn't . . ." she exclaimed, sounding genuinely shocked, and Lou snuggled down into the sofa and closed her eyes.

"I would and I could, and I'm sick of all your play-acting," she said in the tones of someone dismissing a tiresome interruption. "You're a very worthless person, really, Melissa – I can't think why I admired you so much. Go away now. I want to talk to my husband."

Piers, no less than Melissa, was observing his wife with an air of surprise, but in Piers' expression a deep tenderness swallowed up the first astonishment, and Melissa saw it.

"Well," she said, getting to her feet with less than her usual grace of movement, "that seems to be my cue for exeunt all. I take it that your injunction to get out was a figure of speech, Piers – I would prefer the shelter of my bedroom to the doubtful charms of your island weather. I can't, with the best will in the world, walk home in traditional fashion with a stretch of ocean to cross."

"I don't care where you go so long as you keep away from Lou and from me. Tomorrow I'll take you to the mainland no matter what the weather's doing, and if you're sick that's just too bad," Piers said, and watched her move to the door with that deliberate little swing of the hips which he had once found so provocative.

He turned with a sense of release to Lou, his anger forgotten, and thought how like a little contented cat she looked, curled up with boneless grace against the cushions; a little cat that had found its niche at last and, like all its species, taken possession.

He knelt down beside the sofa and dropped a light kiss on her forehead.

"Lou," he said, "I have to go out again. I may be gone

some time."

Her eyes flew open and she looked at him with a flicker of fear. "You're going after Sam?"

"The news isn't good," he told her gently. "The launch has been found – empty."

"Oh, no!" she whispered. It was the culminating horror of the day, the last evil fruits of her cousin's thoughtless machinations – or perhaps it would not be the last.

"Piers, you will take care, won't you?" she said, thinking at the same time what an idiotic thing it was to say. Putting to sea in the teeth of a gale was scarcely on a par with crossing a road safely. He did not, however, seem to consider her request absurd. He took her face between his hands and said gravely:

"You understand I have to go, don't you, Lou? The islanders are my responsibility."

"Yes, of course. Do you think – do you suppose Sam has drowned?"

"One can't possibly conjecture. The launch was drifting close to the mainland, so it's feasible he may have got ashore, but I must make enquiries, do what I can."

"Piers . . ." she said, her arms going round his neck, ". . . come back to me . . ."

He gave her no verbal reassurances but held her hard against him for a moment. He did not say goodbye, and was gone before she had time to struggle off the sofa.

She stood by the window for a long time trying to distinguish a moving figure in the darkness, but either her eyes were not keen enough or he had gone down to the harbour another way. Presently she saw the lights of hurricane lamps bobbing to and fro in the distance and then a stronger beam stretching across the black water growing smaller and fainter as the launch drew away from the island.

The hours of waiting seemed very long. Lou was grateful

for any small chore to occupy her mind, and as the evening passed, it became evident that Tibby was not only relinquishing the household reins for the first time, but was incapable of constructive effort. She sat, an old, bent woman, rocking herself and muttering, and Lou caught snatches of ancient superstitions and island beliefs, and every so often invocations to saints with strange Cornish names to work miracles.

"You'm mistress here now, missis, you'm what he needs, and he knows it," Tibby kept saying. "You'm a good maid, a loving maid, and Tibby was wrong to harm you – mortal wrong. 'Tes a judgment on me if he's taken."

"You haven't harmed me, Tibby," Lou said gently. "You were jealous for another bride, that's all, but she'll be gone soon."

"Gone – aye, Miss Blanche went long ago. Her was never meant for Rune, nor for Piers. He never should have listened to that Jezebel – tempting the spirits for her fancy trash," said Tibby strangely, then suddenly began to talk quite rationally. She went back into the past, it was true, but her speech was perfectly coherent, and Lou could not know that she herself, curled up on the hearth in a dressing-gown, brought back the old nursery days with merciful obliteration of the present.

She told Lou tales of Piers' childhood, dwelling reminiscently on trivial incidents which, until now, she must have almost forgotten, bringing to life a time when the Merricks were ordinary, simple people not yet gilded by the dazzling trappings of wealth and fortune. Listening enthralled, as she would have to any bedtime story of improbable good fortune, Lou began to have another picture of her husband, the picture of a boy who, thrust suddenly into a world of makebelieve no less unexpected than her own, had later sought to escape from his loneliness in the freedom and power that riches could bring him.

"His father died too soon, you see," Tibby said, still rocking gently, "and Piers came too young into the inheritance. 'Tes natural, I suppose, for a young man to let money go to his head for a time, but Piers never squandered, even then. He liked to play with power, maybe, and the world soon taught him that other folks are venial."

"Why do you tell me this, Tibby?" Lou asked.

"Because," Tibby answered, "for all the heartless change in his marriage plans, I think he's chosen right. Yes, missis, I know I gave you no welcome when you came, but my thoughts were mazed with old ties ... Piers never found love because he never looked for it. Women to him were easily come by, and when it came to settling down it was a case of selection and no more. A man, you see, can marry from a sense of duty to the future and not miss the best that's been withheld, but a woman ... a woman needs more, and gives more. You've already given your own heart, haven't you, missis?"

"Oh, yes," said Lou simply. "It isn't difficult to learn to love Piers here on the island."

She scrambled to her feet and limped over to the window to look out. There seemed to be a lull in the storm and the almost forgotten household sounds were loud in the sudden stillness, the ticking of clocks, steam hissing from pots and kettles on the range, and the familiar monotonous creak of Tibby's rocking-chair.

"It's gone quiet suddenly," Lou said. "Could it mean the storm's dying?"

"When the tide's on the turn the weather can change," Tibby answered indifferently. "You'm right, though, 'tes surely quieter. You'd best eat something, missis."

Lou had no appetite for food, but it seemed best to encourage the old servant's return to normality by acquiescing. Melissa, too, could hardly be left to go supperless to bed, but Lou had to prepare a tray and take it up herself. Tibby's hostility which, it would seem, like her strange affections, had to be directed somewhere as an outlet, was focussed now on the guest.

"There's stew in this pot; take her a bowlful of that," she said, beginning to bustle round the kitchen again. "I'll have something more tasty for you when you come back."

Lou ladled the stew into a bowl, sniffing it suspiciously, and Tibby, catching her in the act, gave a harsh chuckle.

"There's nothing in it that would harm a babe," she said, and Lou let out a little sigh of thankfulness that at last the old woman seemed to have accepted her on equal terms.

"You did doctor those potions you gave my cousin, to keep her here, didn't you, Tibby?" she said casually, and Tibby sniffed.

"Aye, I did," she admitted defiantly. " 'Twasn't meant at the time in spite for her, but it pleases me now to think of the vomiting she endured to stop on the island."

"You're a wicked old woman," Lou said, picking up Melissa's tray, and both of them exchanged a smile of mutual respect and liking.

Melissa was not in her own room, but across the passage in Lou's, tearing clothes off their hangers and throwing them into suitcases, the mink coat slung across her shoulders, stoles and fur jackets bunched over her arm. Lou stood in the doorway, watching her, the tray in her hands, and Melissa swung round guiltily.

"Oh, it's you," she said, sounding relieved. "I thought at first it might be Piers."

"Piers," said Lou gravely, "is out in the boat looking for Sam. You don't seem to care, Melissa, that your trivial needs may be costing lives."

"What utter tripe! Sam shouldn't have gone if it wasn't safe, and Piers had no need to go chasing off like a distracted hen."

"You have no sense of values, have you? You couldn't care less what happens so long as you get your favourite brand of cigarettes."

"Really, darling, you're all making a frightful fuss about nothing, and your high-minded husband was damn rude to me. I'm well out of this marriage if it means playing second fiddle to this ghastly island, and you can keep the much publicised Piers Merrick with my blessing."

"Thank you," Lou replied politely. "What are you doing with my clothes?"

"*Your* clothes! I'm helping myself to some of my own trousseau, that's all," snapped Melissa. "I'm going to have something out of this half-baked plan of Blanche's to get herself out of a jam, and you promised me the mink, anyway."

"The mink was a hostage for good behaviour," Lou said with deceptive mildness. "Even you can hardly claim to have played fair. In any case, Piers will have the final say in what you take away tomorrow. For myself, I couldn't care less."

Melissa eyed her doubtfully. Little Cousin Lou who had been of no consequence in their lives for so long looked as dim as usual standing there in her dressing-gown holding a tray like a schoolgirl dispatched on an errand, but there was something about her all the same that gave a belated warning for caution.

"Lou – you've always been generous," she began, her voice softening to the wheedling tones which once had had easy power over her cousin. "You have only to say the word to Piers and he'll eat out of your hand. You've got him where you want – or didn't you know?"

Lou's patience snapped, and with it the good manners she had been trying to hold on to.

"Don't you realize, you bitch, that he may not even come back? That while you're standing here trying to bargain for a few furs and anything else you can get, I'm nearly out of my mind for Piers' safety?" she shouted, and banged the tray down on the nearest table with such violence that Tibby's stew splashed into Melissa's face.

"Here's your supper, and I hope it chokes you! There's no convenient drug in it this time to make you ill, and if there were I'd see you're on that launch tomorrow if it's the last thing I do, and I hope you *are* sick — sick as a dog — !"

She began to run down the stairs, forgetful of her injured ankle until the sudden pain slowed her down and she reached out to the banister for support. The unfamiliar force of her own feelings had shocked her, not only into fresh anxiety for Piers, but the frightening realization of how easily murder might be done in the heat of the moment. She could, she thought, clinging shaking to the banister rail, have choked the life out of her abominable cousin without remorse.

Somewhere in the house a door banged in the wind, the stove in the hall gave out an acrid belch of smoke and Tibby's voice called suddenly from the kitchen.

"Missis . . . missis . . . the launch is putting in. They're back . . . or one of 'em is . . ." Her voice faltered on the last words, and Lou sped down the dimly lit passage to the kitchen, ignoring her aching ankle.

Tibby stood, gaunt and erect at the window. "See," she said, pointing, as Lou joined her. "Lights . . . voices . . . the storm has surely lessened that you can hear the voices . . ."

They stood together, the old woman and the young girl, straining their eyes against the darkness. Lou, in the first great tide of thankfulness that swept over her, could only send wordless thanks to those strange-sounding Cornish saints whom Tibby had invoked so often. She could see the same moving lanterns as before and make out muffled shouts above the abating wind. She could not distinguish returning figures, but Tibby's eyes were quicker from long custom.

"There's only one . . . there's only one of 'em come back . . . 'tes a judgment," she said, and there was a grim acceptance in her voice which quenched for the moment Lou's flood of happiness that the one returning could only be Piers.

She wanted to run to meet him, to have that blessed reunion out there in the anonymous darkness of the island, but she must not abandon Tibby to wait alone for the tidings which Piers would bring. So they still stood together, and even when the front door slammed and a man's firm footstep could be heard on the flags, Lou stayed where she was, resting a comforting hand on the old servant's shoulder.

Piers paused in the doorway, observing them both for a moment in silence. He looked very tired and there was disappointment in the quick glance he gave his wife as if he had expected something else of her. He seemed too weary to discard the wet oilskin that hung loosely from his shoulders, and his sea-boots left little pools of water on the clean kitchen floor.

"Still up, Lou? It's very late," he said tonelessly, and she knew instinctively that he misunderstood her apparent reluctance to run to him, touch him, weep, even in thankfulness for his safe return.

"Sam?" she said, and he became aware then of Tibby's rigidity, and of the mute question in both their faces.

"Sam's all right," he replied. "He was washed ashore with a broken leg which serves him right, but he's sitting very pretty in St. Bede's Cottage Hospital, so now, Cinderella, show a little more enthusiasm for your husband's safe return."

Lou ran to him then, whispering her thankfulness into his damp shoulder, tasting the salt on his lips as she kissed him, groping with eager fingers for the reality of flesh and blood and bone. He saw now the strain in her face, and felt the urgency in the hands which were seeking so feverishly for reassurance, and he held her close against him for a moment, too moved to speak at once.

"Why, Lou ..." he said then, softly, "do you care so much?"

"You shouldn't need to ask me," she answered, forgetting Tibby's presence altogether. "Did you think I had no welcome for you, Piers?"

"No, I suppose I didn't. I've understood very little about you, altogether, I think, Cinderella."

She smiled a little tremulously.

"Are you always going to call me that?"

"Probably. Shall you mind?"

She gave a small sigh.

"Not really, only – "

"Only what?"

"I don't want to stay a story-book character for ever. Even Cinderella, once she had recovered from her rags-to-riches shock, must have expected to be taken seriously by her Prince Charming."

"And don't I take you seriously enough, Lou? I don't flatter myself that I'm any Prince Charming, but at least that gentleman had no doubts to conquer once he saw the slipper fitted."

"What do you mean, doubts?"

"As to whether he'd been fair – as to whether his princess would understand that he was not being tardy or reluctant, but simply anxious to amend his neglected wooing."

She did not answer at once, conscious of the strange quiet. The sudden cessation of the storm seemed to her as miraculous as the promise of felicity which she read in Piers' face. She reached up a hand to brush away the drops of water trickling from his hair, then, remembering now that they were not alone, glanced quickly over her shoulder; but Tibby had gone. She must have slipped away with that noiseless secretiveness which once had seemed so sinister, and Lou gave a little sigh of capitulation.

"I understand now," she said, "for you don't seem a stranger any more. You see, I couldn't help myself falling in love with you, so that when you – "

"When I failed you as a lover and a husband you

thought I was regretting our marriage?"

"Well, yes . . . and then Melissa came . . ."

She saw his face darken and wished she had not chosen that moment to remind him of the bride he should have married, but the mischief Melissa had wrought had to be faced between them some time.

"We will both of us try to forget your cousin," Piers said with the old note of arrogance. "You, having a trusting nature, were scarcely to be expected not to take her at face value, but I should have known better. I apologise, Lou."

"For loving her?"

She was unprepared for the rough shaking he gave her and the savage exasperation which crept into his voice.

"I never loved her, you little fool! It was a marriage of convenience, which I thought everyone understood – Blanche certainly did. Oh, I was sufficiently attracted physically to render the relationship painless while it lasted, but I've felt that way about many women and never loved any of them. I'd come to accept the fact, you see, that honest affection and a great deal of money weren't compatible, and then I had to go and marry you."

He seemed to speak with such resentment that she blinked up at him a little nervously.

"You didn't *have* to," she said, "but now that you have – and now that you say you can't love anyone – "

"Well?"

"It's – it's going to stay that way, that's all. I – I'm old-fashioned, you see."

"Certainly it's going to stay that way – I'm old-fashioned myself, now I think of it – and I didn't say I couldn't love anyone – I simply said I never had. Good grief, Cinderella, do you want things spelt out for you?"

But for the first time she was undisturbed by his quick impatience, for the first time she knew faith in herself as a woman. She lowered her lashes and glanced up at him through them with unconscious invitation.

"If spelling things out means a formal declaration, then I do. Even Cinderella must have been told she was loved at some point in the story," she answered sedately. "Do you know what Tibby said to me? She said 'pleasure him, missis.'"

He looked amused.

"Did she, indeed? That's an expression dating back to the Restoration," he said. "Do you know what it means?"

"What it says, I suppose, and it would — it would pleasure *me* very much, dear, difficult Piers, if you would do a little of that spelling for me."

"And don't you know — even now?"

"Perhaps. Even so it's only polite to put such things into words," she said.

"That," he replied, suddenly catching sight of the time on the kitchen clock, "is pure vanity and not to be indulged at two o'clock in the morning. You're looking worn out, my poor darling, and I must own to being a bit whacked myself, so no more of these rather blatant red herrings."

He saw the momentary disappointment in her face and his smile was tender as he turned her gently round towards the door.

"You shall have all you want of me tomorrow, Cinderella," he said gravely. "I want our uninvited guest out of the house before we begin afresh — do you understand?"

"Yes," she said, and knew that he was right. With Melissa gone the slate would be wiped clean again.

Tomorrow, she thought, drowsily mounting the stairs with Piers' supporting arm about her, the island would regain its magic and work its spell, for of course, it was enchanted. Hadn't she known from the very beginning that it was all a dream?

"I shall wake up, of course," she said, and was unaware that she had spoken aloud until Piers picked her up and carried her the rest of the way, saying:

"You're half alseep already, my poor bemused Cinderella. You'll wake up, I hope, to a happier day. I have a lot of leeway to make up, Lou, a lot of amends before I join you in your fairy tale."

"You're nice ..." she murmured like a pleased child whose makebelieve has been taken seriously, and he laughed. But it was no longer makebelieve, she thought, as he laid her on her bed, even though for her the fairy tale must persist for a time because she was little Louise Parsons to whom nothing exciting ever happened.

"But I'm not – not any more," she said, sitting up on the bed, suddenly very wide awake.

"Not what?" he asked with a lifted eyebrow. "You appear to be having some rather confusing thoughts, or are you dreaming again?"

"Not Louise Parsons."

"No, indeed. You're Louise Merrick – Mrs. Piers Merrick, and don't you forget it."

"I won't," she said, then looked up at him with brave resolve. "Piers, you once told me you never regretted things. If they didn't work out, you said, you just forgot them – or – threw them away."

"Did I say that?"

"Yes, you did – and – and I just want you to know that – that I don't choose to be thrown away like a – like a smelly kipper, or something."

He looked down at her sitting there so upright and defiant in her blue dressing-gown, the childish disorder of her soft, straight hair vying with the generous maturity of her mouth, and his own mouth became infinitely tender.

"A smelly kipper?" he repeated, striving to keep his voice grave. "What a poor conceit you have of yourself, dear, silly Lou. For your information, if it's any comfort, I never throw away something that's worth while. Does that help?"

Her blinking became uncontrollable and she suppressed a tiny yawn. "And I'm worth while?"

"Very much so, darling – but telling you will keep till tomorrow. You're nearly asleep."

"Tomorrow..." she murmured happily, and thought of all the delectable things that would happen tomorrow; Melissa gone, and the storm forgotten. Tibby offering a truce, and Piers ... dear, difficult, bedevilled Piers ready at last to start his wooing ... Tomorrow ...

"Tomorrow," she said, her eyelids beginning to droop, "I'm going to give orders – to have that other bed moved. It's so ridiculous to waste room space when there's no need – isn't it?"

His tired eyes twinkled as he pushed her gently back against the pillows.

"Yes, you do that little thing," he said. "As you so rightly say, it's ridiculous to waste room space. Goodnight, my absurd darling."

His kiss was so light that she scarcely felt it, but she heard the door between their rooms close softly and for the last time. She lay listening with gratitude to the return of the familiar island sounds, the wash of the sea, the faint hoot of a passing vessel, the wind now no more than a gentle accompaniment to sleep ... Piers' escape from the demands of the world, and now hers.

Too tired and too contented to make the effort to get into bed, she curled up among the pillows like the little stray cat that she was and slept.

Other titles available this month in the Mills & Boon Classic Series

SWEET TO REMEMBER
by Anne Weale

When Clive Lister, rich and handsome, came into Deborah's life, John Harriby issued dire warnings about wolfishness. John was prejudiced, because he was in love with Deborah himself, but—could he be right all the same?

MOON OVER AFRICA
by Pamela Kent

Elizabeth's journey to Cape Town included the very reverse of a shipboard romance, for a lively mutual dislike was established between her and a certain tall, dark passenger.

THE GARDEN OF PERSEPHONE
by Nan Asquith

When Stacey was widowed after a year of marriage, she felt that she could never love again. For her small son's sake, she went to visit her rich father-in-law on the Greek island of Melaenus and found herself offered, despite many complications there, the opportunity of another kind of happiness.

35p net each
Available February 1976

Forthcoming Classics

RETURN OF SIMON
by Celine Conway

Simon Leigh's female relatives wanted him to marry and settle down at Craigwood, his family's old home. Why shouldn't he? Women seemed to like him—except Pat Gordon, his sister-in-law's secretary, and she and Simon managed to strike sparks from each other whenever they met!

NO OTHER HAVEN
by Kathryn Blair

When Lindsey was left alone in the world, Stuart Conlowe married her—in name only, he said, until they grew to know each other better. But soon Lindsey found herself fighting bitterly for Stuart's love against the other woman in his life.

WIFE TO CHRISTOPHER
by Mary Burchell

When Christopher discovered how Vicki had tricked him into marrying her he was, not unnaturally, furious and disgusted. By that time, though, Vicki had fallen genuinely in love with him. But how could she persuade him, now, that she could ever make him happy?

FOLLOW A DREAM
by Marjorie Moore

It was a chance meeting with a stranger in Paris that decided Julia to return to England, the land of her childhood—but the stranger was nothing to her, and she was certainly of no importance to him. She was just following a dream. Would anything but disappointment come of it all?

35p net each

Available March 1976

Did you miss any of our recent titles in this series?

WIFE WITHOUT KISSES
by Violet Winspear

Rea went to Hastings for a quiet visit with **no** thought of marriage in her mind, but soon she found herself married to a man she had never met before and pledged to play her part in a fantastic game of "let's pretend".

BLACK CHARLES
by Esther Wyndham

Once in every generation a dark-haired man was born into the traditionally fair-haired Pendleton family. Always they were known as Black Charles, arrogant and fierce men who would never marry. It fell to Audrey Lawrence to cross swords with the latest in the line.

MY DEAR COUSIN
by Celine Conway

Lisa wasn't exactly Adrian's cousin—but there was a family connection which in his view entitled him to summon her to Africa to help him out of a difficulty. He was surprised to find that the schoolgirl he remembered had grown into a young woman with a will of her own.

FLOWERING WILDERNESS
by Kathryn Blair

Nicky was tough enough to endure the climate and discomforts of West Africa, but she could not stand by and see Dave Raynor, whom she loved, being ensnared by a woman who cared only for his money ...

35p net each

Did you miss any of our recent titles in this series?

A COTTAGE IN SPAIN
by Rosalind Brett

Aunt Natalie's legacy of a villa on the Costa Brava was really a thinly-disguised plot to manoeuvre Linda into marrying a charming Spaniard. Linda's English neighbour had charm too; and the situation might have developed as a pleasant, harmless comedy if Maxine had not turned up. For where Maxine went, drama and disaster might easily follow.

THE HOUSE OF SEVEN FOUNTAINS
by Anne Weale

Malaya is the background to this story of a strong-willed girl and an even more strong-willed doctor. From their first meeting he snubbed her and she resented him – but first impressions can often be misleading...

THE RELUCTANT ORPHAN
by Sara Seale

When Julian Dane's first romance went wrong, he said: 'This time ... I'll pick my wife out of an orphanage and see that she has no preconceived notions that interfere with mine.' He was as good as his word, but he had not allowed for Jennet's having a personality of her own.

CAME A STRANGER
by Celine Conway

Tess was resigned to the fact that she must give up her hopes for running a guest house by a lake at the foot of the Rockies and go home to England. What she hadn't expected was that when a buyer for her house materialised, he would try to organise her life as well!

35p net each

Did you miss any of our recent ·
titles in this series?

35p net each